Marquis de Ségur, F. J. M. A Partridge

Gaston De Ségur

A Biography, Condensed From The Memoir

Marquis de Ségur, F. J. M. A Partridge

Gaston De Ségur
A Biography, Condensed From The Memoir

ISBN/EAN: 9783743462960

Printed in Europe, USA, Canada, Australia, Japan

Cover: Foto ©Raphael Reischuk / pixelio.de

Manufactured and distributed by brebook publishing software (www.brebook.com)

Marquis de Ségur, F. J. M. A Partridge

Gaston De Ségur

GASTON DE SEGUR

A BIOGRAPHY

Condensed from the French Memoir

BY

THE MARQUIS DE SEGUR

BY

`F J M A PARTRIDGE

LONDON

BURNS AND OATES

GRANVILLE MANSIONS W

1884

✠

DOMINUS ILLUMINATIO MEA

ET SALUS MEA

QUEM TIMEBO

DOMINUS PROTECTOR VITÆ MEÆ

A QUO TREPIDABO

(Psalm xxvi.*)*

PREFACE.

THE following work, like some others which have appeared in the same Series, is neither an original nor a translation. It has been freely condensed from the extremely interesting work of the Marquis de Ségur, *Souvenirs d'un Frère*. It is hoped however, that nothing of importance in the life of Mgr. de Ségur has been passed over, and that these pages may serve to place before English Catholics the main features of the career of one of the noblest souls of our time, whom most of us must often have heard of, and whom some may have had the privilege of knowing.

Force and simplicity were the characteristics of Gaston de Ségur. His life was one of singular devotion, energetic piety, and Christian manliness, and His Master loved him too much not to give him a large share of the Cross. He bore it in a manner that ensured his sanctification, while at the same time he made it only one reason more for exerting himself to the utmost in the cause of religion and charity. The large fruits which were gathered in for the glory of God and the good of souls by this 'Blind Apostle' form the most significant and consoling features of a saintly career.

H. J. C.

III *Mount Street :*
Feast of St. Mary Magdalene, 1884.

CONTENTS.

CONTENTS.

CHAPTER I.

Childhood, Youth, and Early Manhood.

GASTON DE SEGUR was born in Paris on the 15th
of April, 1820.   He was the eldest child of his
parents, the Comte and Comtesse de Ségur, and
was welcomed into the world with great rejoicing,
not only by them but by his grand-parents, all of
whom were living at the time.   His maternal
grandfather, in particular, Count Rostopchine, was
made very proud and happy by this first grandchild,
who was, indeed, an important person at that time,
when peerages were hereditary in France.   In a
letter to his son-in-law, when the heir of the house
was barely a year old, the grandfather begs "to
kiss the feet of Gaston, the premier paladin of
Christendom."

Nothing in the traditions of his family, in the
spirit of the age, nor in his early training, contained
a prophecy of Gaston de Ségur's future.   But we
may well believe that it was influenced in no small
degree by the prayers of his holy grandmother, the
Countess Rostopchine, who was also his godmother,
and to whose counsels and example he attributed a
large share in the great work of his conversion.

B

Gaston was placed, when hardly more than an infant, at a school, the solitary merit of which, according to his biographer, was the pure air in which it was situated. Till the law of 1850, the best that could be done was to choose an establishment not positively bad. It is not then wonderful that, in spite of the blessing of a Christian home, Gaston's school-days, both at this time and later on in Paris, bear no mark whatever of the supernatural. The two strongest feelings of his nature were love for his mother, so strong as to be almost a passion, and love for painting, which would doubtless have been his vocation, had not God chosen him for higher things. Indeed, drawing became before long his chief occupation, and encroached so largely on the time supposed to be devoted to his studies, as to be a fruitful source of impositions. These last, however, he frequently induced his masters to commute for a portrait or a sketch, a plan which, no doubt, possessed the rare merit of pleasing all parties, but which can hardly have had the effect of weaning the culprit from the illicit pleasure.

From his earliest childhood, the boy's love for his mother was characterised by a strength and a delicacy which are remarkable. At eight years old, when his brother is about to join him at school, he writes to her that he is "both glad and sorry—glad because I shall see him—sorry because he will not see you." Thoughtful tenderness for her breathes in every line of his boyish letters. He asks her to be more prudent about her health, not to treat his letters as a joke, but to remember that her future belongs to her children. When the little sister, Olga, begins to run alone, he rejoices that now his mother need not make her arms ache with carrying her. He envies two of his friends who are leaving school because they will be with their mother, "the best mother but one in the world." Only once is there the shadow of a cloud between the mother and son. The boy had not been quite frank about some trifling matter, and the Countess, prizing as she must have done the great treasure of her child's confidence, writes to reprove him with what seems almost too great severity. Gaston's reply begins by thanking her for her letter and for her advice: he acknowledges his fault with child-like simplicity, asks her pardon in all humility, and ends with an assurance that he loves her better than ever, "if that is possible." How many lads of seventeen, on the point of leaving school, would receive a rebuke for a far graver fault in such a spirit? But in all these letters, so charming in their affection and unselfishness, there is no trace whatever of religious principle. They are the outcome of a sweet and generous nature, but the Christian spirit is altogether latent.

During all the long period, twelve years, of Gaston de Ségur's school-life, there seems to have been but one event which was distinctly Christian. But then that exception was his First Communion !

He was prepared for that great act by the curé of the village where his first school was situated, a good and zealous priest, who did his utmost for God in evil days and in a difficult position, and for whom Mgr. de Ségur always cherished a filial affection. The venerable old man, when more than eighty years old, was a frequent and honoured guest at his table, and it was to the sincere piety with which he received his God for the first time that Gaston always ascribed the grace of his conversion. This last event took place in the year 1838, when his grandmother Rostopchine came to pass the summer at Les Nouettes, the happy country home of the Ségur family. Gaston was there for his vacation, and seems to have yielded instantly to the holy attraction exercised over him by that great soul, and from this moment he determined to give himself altogether and for ever to God. His family noticed and wondered at the change in him. It was a complete transformation. He prepared by a general confession for the Communion which he had resolved should be the beginning of a new life, and on the feast of our Lady's Nativity, in the lowly church of the little parish of Aube, "Jesus Christ," to borrow the words of the Marquis de Ségur, "entered his soul as' a Conqueror Who was never again to leave it."

The following extract from a letter addressed to her grandson by the Countess Rostopchine on his entering the Seminary, seems to come in naturally at this point of Gaston's life :

My good and dear godson,—I am not sure that you are not mistaken in giving me credit for so large a share in the work of your return to the truth. That truth, either through your own fault or that of your instructors, was unknown to you, but the love of it was in your heart, though unconsciously, up to the moment when a ray of it was revealed to you by the Infinite Goodness. You followed it at once ; I found the faith planted in you, the mustard-seed watered, and as God makes use of men to help His children, I said something to you of what I had learnt myself, a good deal later than you,[1] and introduced you to some good books, but I should not have done or helped on anything, if God had not already undertaken the work Himself. My numerous failures in regard to others prove to me what an empty sound the human voice is, by itself. Prayer is a help, no doubt, but only to those whose dispositions do not make prayer powerless. My success is due to your dispositions, and those dispositions were the fruit of God's grace.

Gaston's time was now divided between his family, his art, and works of charity. He found out a way of practising these last even when, from time to time, in order to please his mother, he appeared in society, and looked out for girls without friends, with

[1] Madame Rostopchine was a convert from the Greek Schismatic Church.

whom he danced "charity-dances." Many of his evenings were passed in his grandmother's room, and conversation went on pleasantly while he drew. But before long a weakness in the eyes obliged him to lay aside his pencil—it was the first warning of the trial which was to be the sanctification of his life.

This first attack was soon over, and after a short rest, Gaston began to attend Delaroche's studio, but the freedom of manners and conversation, and the necessity of working from nude models so disgusted him, that after a few months, with many regrets, he broke off his studies there. His models, chiefly children and old men, used to come to his rooms to sit. We are told that while judges of art gave high praise to the heads, hands, and feet of his figures, they missed the play of the muscles, the accuracy of form which should have been evident under the drapery. An amusing incident of this is related with regard to a portrait which he painted of Pius the Ninth between SS. Peter and Paul, on examining which the Pope exclaimed: "Why, this good M. de Ségur has forgotten to give us any shoulders!"

Gaston de Ségur continued to be on intimate terms with Delaroche, who was always ready to advise him. He was a frequent visitor at his house, and a great favourite with the artist's charming wife, of whom he used to speak as of an angel whom God had allowed to spend a short time on earth. Gaston's favourite subjects, as might be supposed, were religious, but he had a gift for portrait-painting, and, it must be confessed, for caricatures. He was careful, however, not to pass the limits of harmless fun, and if now and then his keen sense of the ridiculous carried him too far, the mischievous production was speedily destroyed.

But while cultivating the talent God had given him, and attending conscientiously to the studies which were to prepare him for his future career, Gaston's heart was given to God and His poor. The Conference of St. Vincent de Paul to which he belonged numbered many fervent members, among whom was Pierre Olivaint. One beautiful practice they had adopted was to make pilgrimages to the well-nigh deserted churches in the neighbourhood of Paris, going to hear Mass in parties of three or four, now in one, now in another, with the holy intention of re-kindling the faith of the people, and bringing hope and comfort to their discouraged pastors.

Gaston had a particular affection for the aged poor, and they in their turn, welcomed his visits as they did those of a sunbeam to their miserable garrets. Long years after this time, the mere mention of his name was enough to light up the faces of the old friends he used to visit. His usual associate in hospital visiting was young Olivaint, with whom he took days and hours in turn, true precursors of our Lord for Whose coming to the souls of the sick and dying they prepared the way.

One incident of his hospital visiting we give in his own words :

The ward I had to visit that day was under the charge of a Sister of Charity, who had grown old in this admirable work, and was as unwearied in soothing the sufferings of her patients as she was zealous for the good of their souls. 'Go to No. 39,' she said to me, 'a man of two or three-and-thirty, in the last stage of consumption, who has only a day or two to live. I can do nothing with him, try as I may—nor the Chaplain either, and one of your brothers of St. Vincent de Paul (it was Pierre Olivaint) has succeeded no better. He will very likely send you about your business, but all the same we must try everything—it is a poor soul to be saved.'

'Oh, my dear Sister, if he sends me about my business I must just go, that is all—it will do me no harm. Only say a Hail Mary for the poor fellow while I speak to him.' . . . . .

When I came to his bed he fixed his eyes on me without speaking. I asked him how he felt—no answer. 'Are you in much pain just now ? Can I do anything for you?' Not a word. Things were becoming embarrassing, the man's looks were more and more threatening, and I expected him to say something abusive. All at once God, in His Providence, sent me an inspiration.

I came close to the poor fellow and whispered, 'Did you make a good First Communion?' The effect was like an electric shock—his expression changed, and he murmured rather than said: 'Yes, sir.' 'Well, my friend, and were you not very happy in those days?' Again he said, 'Yes, sir,' in a trembling voice, and I saw two big tears roll down his cheeks.

I took his hands in mine: 'And why were you happy then, but because you were innocent and chaste—because you feared God—in a word, because you were a good Christian! That happiness may be yours again; the good God has not changed.' He continued to weep. 'You will make your confession, will you not?' 'Yes, sir,' he answered firmly, holding out his arms to me. I embraced him with all my heart and gave him a little advice to help him in his good resolution. Then I left him, and went to tell the Sister of my unexpected success.

This was the first soul, so far as we know, which Gaston de Ségur won to God.

As soon as his studies were completed, Gaston paid a long visit to the Countess Rostopchine at the palace near Moscow, made memorable by the act of her late husband, who burnt down the original building with his own hands, that it might not fall into the hands of Napoleon. It had been rebuilt, and here the widow passed most of her life in retirement and prayer. The intimate intercourse during two months with this strong and holy soul was not only a spiritual consolation, but a real help in the spiritual life. Madame Rostopchine was a wonderful woman in many ways; and her strength of character, profound learning, and austere life, made her more like a Christian of the age and the stamp of St. Paula and Olympias than a pious woman of the nineteenth century.

Gaston returned to France only to prepare for another journey; this time to Rome, where his father, anxious to give scope to his artistic vocation, had obtained for him the post of *attaché* to M. de Latour-Maubourg, the French Ambassador at the Holy See, and an old friend of the family. Before leaving France he was told that a portrait of his father which he had exhibited was judged worthy of the gold medal—a great honour for a young artist. On his return from Rome in 1843 his mother placed the medal in his hands, and he kept it for a month or two, before entering the Seminary, as a *souvenir* of his brief art-career. But, pressed by the charity of Christ, the one Love of his heart, he sold the medal before long, and to Christ, in the person of His poor, he gave the price.

The year which followed was—need it be said?— a very happy one to the young Christian artist; his colleagues, too, all agreeable, and several brilliant and distinguished, were men of whom he always retained an affectionate remembrance. There was the Comte de Rayneval, first secretary to the Embassy, and afterwards the courageous advocate of the union of the French government with the Holy See. He was a first-rate musician, and a brilliant performer, a great attraction to a lover of music like Gaston, and they were soon fast friends. We can do no more than mention the names of

Just de Latour-Maubourg, the nephew of his chief, a frank bright spirit who was the life of the circle; of the Baron de Malaret, an old friend of his childhood and his future brother-in-law, and of the brilliant but eccentric Comte de Cambise.

Gaston's duties were light enough and left him plenty of leisure for society and for the paintings and other treasures of Rome. We will just glance at his artistic occupations and tastes, otherwise our sketch would lack some characteristic touches, since with Gaston de Ségur, next to the service of God— needless to say, after a long interval—came the love and study of his favourite art. Every day he visited some museum or gallery, public or private. Among the antique statues of the Vatican, we learn that he most admired the Demosthenes, which he pre- ferred even to the Apollo Belvedere and the Laocoon. He never could care for Michael Angelo's Moses, whose grand proportions and majestic limbs did not reconcile him to the lack of a supernatural and religious expression. His favourite painter was Perugino, some of whose Madonnas he considered even more heavenly than his great pupil's, but he used to say, for all that, that he believed the Madonna di Foligno to be the first picture in the world. The Marquis thinks that he might have said the *second,* had he ever seen the Madonna di San Sisto.

All this time his pencil was not idle. His talent for caricature proved something of a cross, as *bon gré mal gré* he had to devote most of the evenings spent at the Embassy to its exercise. The Ambassadress, her friends, the other *attachés*, all clamoured for something, and the young artist found it sometimes anything but easy to indulge his sense of humour without offending against charity. He made numerous sketches of a more serious character, and painted one or two large pictures. One of these, a shepherd-lad, studied from nature, his brother considers his best work—and thereby hangs the following tale.

The day after the closing of the Exhibition, where this picture had been much admired, a very deaf Englishman, whose French was hard to understand, called at the house of Madame de Ségur and asked to see the artist. He was out, so the visitor was received by one of Gaston's brothers. On being shown into the *salon* the first thing the Englishman saw was the picture. He stood before it in mute admiration for some time, and then enquired the price. He was told that it was not for sale, but it was some time before he gave up the struggle—he begged it to be understood that he was a very rich man, that he really must have that picture and that he cared nothing what he paid. When at length he was obliged to go, he insisted on leaving his address in case the family should think better of it. At this time Gaston had resolved to enter the Seminary, and the Marquis thinks that had he been at home he would have taken the Englishman at his word and made him pay very dear for the picture, the price of which would have gone to the poor.

M. de Ségur was deeply impressed by the grand figure of Gregory XVI—but he scarcely saw him except during public functions and ceremonies, so that he could not feel for him the devoted personal affection and filial tenderness with which his successor inspired him.

His most cherished friend in Rome, and the one who made his vocation to the priesthood clear to him, was Père de Villefort, of the Society of Jesus, the friend, guide, and director of all the French who visited the tomb of St. Peter, whether as pilgrims or mere travellers. Prejudices against the Society were rife at the time, but they were always laid aside in the case of this Jesuit, often, it may be remarked, the only one the objector had ever known. From the first, Gaston de Ségur gave him his full confidence, but neither director nor penitent was disposed to act hastily, and there was, for several months, no outward sign of any change of plan. Two events hastened matters, a serious illness and a pilgrimage to Loreto. Gaston fell sick at a time when Rome was nearly empty, and the French Embassy nearly deserted, so that the young *attaché* might have fared ill but for the charity of a French priest, the Abbè Véron, who heard of his state, had him moved to his own quarters, and nursed him with the greatest devotion. He con-

tinued the guest of the good Abbé till his health
was quite restored, and the counsels and example of
his new friend, together with the silent but
powerful influence of sickness and suffering,
combined to help on the work already begun in
his soul.

It was early in September when a friend who,
like Gaston, had one foot in and the other out of
the world, asked him to join him in a journey to
Perugia, Assisi, and Loreto, and he left the sanctuary of the Holy House no longer his own, but
pledged for ever in heart and soul to Christ. Three
months later, at the Christmas midnight Mass in the
Gesù, Gaston de Ségur bound himself by a vow of
perpetual chastity, and solemnly promised to
follow his holy vocation. He was not quite twenty-
three years old, and for four years, since his conversion at Aube, he had led a life of Christian holiness
and penance.

He wrote at once to announce his resolution to
his parents. Perhaps the severest trial of his life
was the anguish, almost despair, of his mother on
learning it. Good and pious as she was, she was
so blinded by her passionate affection for him, that
she could not believe in his vocation, which she
persisted in regarding as a delusion sure to pass
away, and she did all in her power to shake his
determination. Letter followed letter, filled with
love so intense, and supplications so heart-breaking,
that Gaston, although he never wavered, was

almost crushed by the thought of the pain he was causing to the mother he adored. He never dared to open her letters till he was on his knees before the Blessed Sacrament, and there he read them, he said, "as one would read the last will of a dying mother." It was very long before Madame de Ségur could reconcile herself to the vocation of her eldest and best-loved child. She herself, when anguish had given place to resignation, and resignation had become an ever-deepening joy, would dwell in her humility on the wild thoughts, born of her blind love, which tortured her even while looking on his calm happy countenance and listening to his cheerful words, when she went to see him at the Seminary. She would confess, when striving to strengthen and comfort some poor mother under a like trial, that there were moments when she found herself half wishing to find her son dead or dying. And yet— this son, whom she thought she was losing, was more with her than any other of her children, more her own than any of them, though wholly given to God; and she saw how, even as regards this world, he had chosen the better part in giving up all for Him. "Seek ye therefore first the kingdom of God and His justice, and all these things shall be added unto you."

Gaston greatly desired to remain at Rome for his ecclesiastical studies, but his parents opposed his wish, and he returned to Paris in the January of 1843. In the summer of this year he paid a farewell visit to his grandmother, the only one of his family who had rejoiced from the first at his resolution; and then followed the last weeks at Les Nouettes.

At this time Gaston received the following from P. de Villefort, whom he had begged to give him some spiritual direction for his life in the Seminary, a letter which is, as the Marquis says, full of interest both for its wisdom and piety and for the high testimony it bears to Saint-Sulpice.

Rome, 25th September 1843.

My very dear Friend,

Ernest de Rayneval has faithfully discharged his commission, and I have already learnt from him that all the dreaded obstacles have been cleared away in a manner which leaves no doubt of the very special protection of God Who is full of mercy and goodness. Your letter confirms the good news and also tells me the time of your entrance into the Seminary. May our Lord be blessed for it !

You did wisely in yielding to your father's wishes with regard to the choice of a confesssor after your return from Rome. It is Jesus Christ Whom we ought always to see in the minister of the Sacrament of reconciliation. Besides, as it will one day be your lot to guide souls, it is profitable for you to be able to judge by experience of the advantages or disadvantages of different sorts of direction. So truly may we say with the Apostle, *Diligentibus Deum omnia cooperantur in bonum.* Yes, my dear friend, let us love God—

love Him with our whole heart and then everything
will help you to love Him more and more.

You wish for some advice as to the details of a
perfect seminarian's life, as to the general spirit which
should inspire his actions and be the mainspring of
his conduct. My dear friend, you are at the fountain-
head of good counsel. You remember, no doubt, what
I have so often said to you about Saint-Sulpice, as
much from spontaneous affection of heart as to combat
the prejudices which you have heard others express.
I now repeat it to you once more—acquire the spirit
which the directors of that school will impart to you,
and you cannot go astray. It is the wise direction
which formed the Venerable de Lasalle, the Venerable
Grignon de Montfort and many others who, after
having continually shed abroad the sweet savour of
Jesus Christ throughout all their priestly career, died
with their hands full of merits and with the reputation
of consummate holiness. The spirit of Saint-Sulpice
is the spirit of Jesus Christ.

The spirit, the perfect life of the seminarian, should
be studied in the Hidden Life of our Lord. Place
before you that sweet Saviour at your age—follow all
His footsteps from His rising to His lying down.
Represent to yourself this God Who is your Pattern,
praying—and strive to pray like Him—working, or
listening to the doctors and asking them questions—
work, listen and enquire like Him and for Him. Ask
yourself how He behaved Himself at meal-times—how
He received the strangers who came to St. Joseph's
workshop—how He conversed with the other youths

C

of Nazareth, without a trace of gloominess or excite‑ ment, or contentiousness or argument—*Arundinem quas‑ atam non confringet.* Study this life of our Lord con‑ tinually in the Seminary, especially His obedience, and think how, though eaten up by the zeal of His Father's house, He kept silence for thirty years. Yes, my dear friend, I am not afraid to assure you, that if, during your years of preparation for the priesthood, it is your chief care to conform yourself to the Hidden Life of Jesus, by copying its virtues, so simple and amiable, so sweet and winning in their manifestation, but requiring an abnegation the greater and more incessant the less it is perceived ; you will, when the time comes for exercising your sacred ministry, repro‑ duce in yourself the virtues of our Saviour's apostolic life. Is there—can there be anything else for us to wish for ?

These are not the words of a man who has even the shadow of a doubt as to your vocation. They pre-suppose a deep conviction of its reality. If, there‑ fore, when you are preparing to enter the seminary, the devil should suggest to you any temptation of melancholy, disgust, or depression, rejoice in being thus conformed to the likeness of our Divine Saviour, Who, on the eve of His Passion, "began to grow sorrowful and to be sad;" only say, too, with Him, "Rise, let us go." Never disturb yourself about any ideas which may occur to you with regard to your vocation. You must have no doubt—absolutely none —on this subject.

We poor Jesuits are a good deal attacked just now.

Pray that we may profit by these trials. I do not believe that you will ever be the victim of the prejudices which some—even good persons—have against us. You know us : and they know us too at Saint-Sulpice. Remember me very particularly in the Loreto chapel at Issy.

PH. DE. VILLEFORT,

of the Society of Jesus.

CHAPTER II.

First years of Priesthood.

IN the October of 1843, Gaston de Ségur entered the
Seminary at Issy, where the young clerics of Saint
Sulpice went through their course of philosophy.
The following year he received the tonsure at the
latter Seminary, then, year after year, minor orders,
the sub-diaconate and diaconate. Over-work had
brought on another attack in his eyes in the course
of this time, but a journey to the north of Italy and
the Tyrolese Alps completely recruited his health,
and in the December of 1849 he was ordained
priest by Mgr. Affre, and the next morning said his
first Mass at our Lady's altar in Saint-Sulpice. His
mother, to whom he hastened after his ordination,
to give her his first blessing, his father, and nearly
all his family, surrounded the altar and received
Holy Communion from his hand. To some of his
friends he confided afterwards a secret which they
kept till after his death: when holding in his hand
for the first time the Sacred Body of his Lord, he
begged His Blessed Mother to obtain from her Son,
as the special grace and benediction of his priesthood, whatever infirmity would be the greatest trial

and daily crucifixion of his nature without diminish‹
ing his usefulness. During the first years of his
priesthood he used to say to those who were in the
secret, "It seems as if I had given our Lady a
tough problem to solve."

Determined to show that, before all things, he
was a priest, the Abbé de Ségur took a little
apartment in the Rue de Grenelle, only joining his
family at dinner. Very soon, however, he left it in
order to live in community with a few other devoted
priests in the Rue Cassette. His first four companions, one of whom was the Abbé Gay, all
belonged to wealthy families, and all agreed that
poverty and simplicity, like those of the religious life,
was one of the first conditions of success among
the poor.

At this time Mgr. Affre was anxiously seeking for
a priest, free from any charge and full of zeal for
souls, to devote himself as voluntary chaplain to
the military prisoners of the Abbaye, whose forlorn
condition appealed powerfully to his fatherly heart.
Mgr. de Ségur eagerly embraced this opportunity of
self-devotion, and the relations between him and
the poor soldiers were very soon of the closest kind.
It was so easy to make confession to this young
priest, who met them with open arms and a heart
overflowing with compassion; and after receiving
absolution, these poor fellows, who had been led
astray by drunkenness, passion, or human respect
(and there are scarcely any but these in military

prisons), returned with joy to the God Whom they had not approached, perhaps, since their First Communion. Many—and they were among the most fervent—received Him now for the first time. The tie thus formed between the priest whom, in spite of his youth, they affectionately called their father, and these prodigals of the army, was not broken when the latter left the Abbaye, either acquitted or condemned; and he received letters from many of them, sometimes sixteen and twenty years later. It is hard to choose among the touching specimens given by the Marquis: here is one from the *Bagne* of Toulon.

"My dear benefactor,—If your charity came from human motives, I might fear that my silence would give you a bad idea of me. I remember when I was alone at the Abbaye, without any one to show me a kindness, you were the only one who brought hope to my soul. . . . It is all as clear to me as if it had just happened, and I keep most carefully everything you gave me—your good books, your medals. Believe me, M. l'Abbé, in this hell upon earth called the *Bagne*, this gulf where everything holy is swallowed up, I need the remembrance of your wise counsels to keep me from the moral contagion so easily caught."

A year later the same man writes to take leave of the Abbé before being sent to Guiana:

"I can only turn to God and to the Blessed Virgin, the Mother of the afflicted, to help me out of this abyss of misery. *There is not a moment of the day that I do not think of our Lord.* I approach the sacraments whenever I can. You ask me if I have your *Imitation* still. Indeed I have, and I shall keep it all my life in remembrance of the good Abbé, who led me out of a bad way and set me in the right one."

Once an old sergeant, named Herbuel, was brought to the Abbaye. He had shot his commanding officer dead out of revenge for some punishment he had inflicted. He became sincerely penitent, received the sacraments with deep devotion, and seemed to have but one desire, that of living a little longer to do penance. His wish was granted. He was condemned to death, but his execution was delayed for two months—two months of agony, but a truly Christian one. "My good M. de Ségur," he wrote to the young chaplain, who was absent for a few days, "I have just had the pleasure of receiving your words of comfort and encouragement. You are always with your children even when absent, always thinking of their good, I keep myself ready and prepared to appear before our Supreme Judge, in Whom is all my confidence. Every day I can face my position better, and when the time comes there will be an end of earthly troubles. My soul is at peace. I only hope I may live long enough for you to be able to give some more consolation to your most respectful Herbuel."

He was executed on All Souls' Day. "God's

will be done," he said when the news was announced. M. de Ségur heard his confession, gave
him the Holy Viaticum, and, when he came to
accompany him to Vincennes, where he was to be
shot, the priest was pale and agitated, the criminal
calm and cheerful. "I cannot tell you what I feel,"
he said, taking the crucifix in his hand; "here is
my Lord Who died for me—now I am going to die
with Him." The old soldier asked and obtained
the favour of giving the word of command—"Fire!"
"I had courage for the crime," he said, "now I
must have it for the expiation. Then, when the
Abbé had given him the last blessing, he cried with
a loud voice, "See, comrades, do not do as I did:
respect your officers. Here is the image of our
Lord Jesus Christ—remember, comrades, I die a
Christian."

Another soldier, named Guth, condemned for a
similar crime, made as good an end. His captain,
whom he had killed, was a fervent Christian who
prayed with his last breath for his murderer's conversion. The first time that this man received
Holy Communion in prison, he nearly fainted from
emotion, and thenceforth he lived only in and for
God. He refused to appeal against his sentence.
"It is just," he said—"I cannot go against God's
law. I would not accept a pardon if I had the
choice. My punishment must expiate my crime."

When the Abbé took his place beside him in the
van which was to convey him to the place of execu-

tion, Guth whispered, " I hardly like to say it, but I feel as if I were going to a wedding." Arrived at Satory, his sentence was read to him. " I acknowledge the justice of my punishment," he said; " I beg pardon of God ; I love Him with all my heart." Then, after embracing the young priest, he knelt down, extended his arms in the form of a cross, and his last words were: " I unite my death to that of my Lord."

It was M. de Ségur who accompanied the murderers of General de Bréa (he was assassinated in 1848) to the scaffold. Two of the number obtained a commutation of their sentence—their names were Chopart and Noury. The former was a young man of much character and intelligence ; he corresponded with the Abbé de Ségur till his death, and his letters are so full of interest, so touching and instructive, that we shall insert some of them here.

Bagne, Rochfort,
July 14*th,* 1849.

Dear Father,—Do not think that my long silence is due to negligence or forgetfulness: but a feeling of shame comes over me whenever I write to you. ' What right,' I ask, ' have I, a man condemned to the galleys, to take up the time and thoughts of those who have protected me—nay, saved my life ? I am to end my days at the *Bagne.* I ought, then, to submit to the fate of being forsaken by every one.' Such thoughts as these, Father, keep coming into my head, the head

so dearly bought, in my moments of weariness and
depression. In a position like mine, though one may
keep from falling, it is impossible in spite of all one's
courage, not to waver—to lose heart. You know,
Father, that I am speaking the truth. You knew me
at a very critical time of my life: then I should have
had the courage to die: then, but for you (who
obtained a commutation of my sentence) I should
have died *game*, as the saying is: after your pious
instructions, so full of gentleness and force, I should
have died like a Christian.

Now, Father, God is trying me in a more terrible
way than in March. The June prisoners condemned
to the galleys are going to Mont Saint-Michel: those
concerned in the Bréa affair, and those guilty of theft,
arson, and murder, remain at the *Bagne*. It is not for
me to complain of this rule: only, Father, I must
repeat what I said at Vanves. I would a hundred
times rather die than be in the position which I owe
to the President's clemency. . . . Physically, I do not
deny it, things are not much better at Saint-Michel
than here: there is, indeed, still less liberty, for here
we work in the harbour together with free labourers.
But, oh! the moral suffering which goes with this
degree of liberty! Every day, every moment, we are
obliged to hear the infamous conversation of our
fellow-prisoners, and, in spite of one's self, gradually
one gets less horrified at it.

At Mont Saint-Michel it is very different in this respect. It is a military prison, and you who are a Chaplain of a similar establishment, know better than any one

that the poor fellows are condemned to hard labour for small offences. I have heard you say yourself that they are very far from devoid of all good sentiments. Let me say a few words about one peculiarity of the men sentenced to the galleys. When the worst of them are sentenced to solitary confinement, they do all they can to get sent to the *Bagne.* They stop at nothing to gain their object, not even at the assassination of a comrade or a warder. . . . In addition to the measure of liberty allowed at the *Bagne*, this preference is attributable to the fixed idea of all *forçats*, that it is easier to escape there than from a central establishment, and escape is the hobby of all of them. No one does escape, as a matter of fact ; but they are not discouraged by that, and, as a rule all the *forçats* are in favour of the attempt. You know, Father, how far I am from thinking in this way. To desire the success of such an attempt would be to wish for theft and murder ; and thank God, I am not fallen so low as that. I have to keep my ideas to myself, from considerations of personal safety, or I should pass for an informer, and no one who is known as such is allowed to live. . . And now, dear Father, having tried to give you a sketch of our life, physically and morally, I come to the object of my letter. I have a great favour to ask of your Christian charity, or rather two favours, for I am not the only one who needs you. That poor mad young fellow, Noury, to whom you, too, were attached, in spite of his strange disposition, has only me to care for him, to encourage him to behave well, nay, even to hope. Besides God there is no one else. He has been

entrusted to me by you and by his sister. Placed as I
am, I regard it as a mission, which I have accepted in
the fullest sense of the words, and with God's help I
will fulfil all the duties it involves. You know, Father,
what this poor lad of eighteen is, who has gained such
a sad celebrity from a few words spoken when he was
not himself. . . . You know how much timidity there is
about him—what a child he is. Why, when he was
condemned to death, and every one imagined him a
fellow of fierce sanguinary appearance, he spent his
time in playing with a pigeon, or on a bad accordion !

The Gospel says: ' Ask, and it shall be given unto
you ; knock and it shall be opened unto you': and so,
Father, I beg you to try to get us sent from the *Bagne*
to another prison. General de Montholon has been
here, and he inquired what characters were borne by
the insurgents left at the *Bagne.* M. le Commissaire
was so kind as to send for me and. to say that he
should give me a very good one. His last words
were: ' Write to M. de Ségur; he has stood your friend
formerly, and he will do so now.' This is why I have
no hesitation in applying to you, and I know well that
if you do not succeed in making things better for us,
it will be because it is impossible. I have had the
happiness of learning what you are, and I know that
you have a deep, true, above all a Christian affection
for me ; and that is the only sort of affection I believe
in now.

My dearest Father, if, after all your endeavours
(you see I have such confidence in you, that before
you have consented to my request I speak as if the

thing was done) you should only obtain the permission for me, then I entreat you to refuse it, otherwise I should be more unhappy than before. If Noury were left to himself, he would go quite mad or kill himself, and then I should reproach myself all my life. Our hearts and prayers will follow you, Father, and may God prosper your endeavours! . . . We have been both saving up for three months, so as to send you a little straw box for your mother. We think it very pretty, and we shall be delighted if your good mother likes it. We would send her something better, but we are not rich, and I know what you look to is the intention, not the value of the gift.

My good Father, when you have a few minutes to bestow on us, write us one of your kind and holy letters. And do not fear, whatever may be the result of your attempt, I will receive good or bad news with faith : *fiat voluntas Tua*. We beg you to remember us in your prayers, and unworthy of it as we are—in the Holy Sacrifice. Dear Father, accept the respectful greetings of your two sons in Jesus Christ,

ANDRE CHOPART.

JEAN NOURY.

The Abbé's efforts were unsuccessful. God had accepted the simple self-sacrificing devotion of His poor child in the *Bagne :* and who shall say how many were the graces with which He rewarded it ? André Chopart remained where he was till a new law allowed him to choose between the *Bagne* and transportation to French Guiana. The young man gladly embraced the latter course, and we now give the letter he wrote to M. de Ségur on the eve of departure, and one written from Cayenne :

Rochefort, May, 1852.

Dear M. l'Abbé,—It is so long since I wrote, that my letter will surprise you. How often must you, who have been so good to me, have accused me of ingratitude. For three years I have lived on delusions, and nothing short of the inscrutable mystery of recent events could have opened my eyes. And yet there has been a bright side to these unrealities on which I have fed for three years : they at least helped to keep me from being corrupted. I was too much absorbed by my *fetishism* to think of anything else. Now that my delusions are over and destroyed, nothing but reality is left : and—oh, my God! what a reality! I have caught at the only plank of salvation which was within my reach in this moral shipwreck of thought and hope. In a few days I sail for Guiana. Had I remained at the *Bagne,* I tell you plainly, Father, I never would have been a Christian. Knowing by bitter experience what the *religiosity* of the *forçats* is, I never would have had part in the monstrous things which go on there. I know quite well that I am not responsible for the sinful actions of others, and yet, I repeat, *I never would have been a Christian* at the *Bagne.* Oh, my Father, if you knew as I do what that terrible life is, perhaps you would wonder less at my obstinacy.

In Guiana, my conduct here, added to the kind-

ness of M. le Commissaire, places me in the first class,
and relying on the promises of the Government, I
may hope, being in this class, to be free some day. . . .
As the time of departure draws nearer, the religious
sentiments, which, thank God, were ineffaceably
engraved on my soul in my youth, become stronger.
I shall have a month to spend on that vast ocean,
which will bring before me the infinite power of its
Creator, and I shall have time to contrast with it the
infinite littleness of men and their works. I do hope
to make a Christian use of my voyage, and to
arrive on the other side regenerated and purified. I
believe, Father, that you will see nothing in my letter
but what I mean it to express—sincerity and a good
resolution.

Would it be too much to ask you sometimes,
when you are able, to answer the letters which I hope
to write you from Guiana?

It is natural to feel, and I do feel pain at leaving
my mother and sister, at putting eighteen hundred
leagues between my native land and the one I am
going to: but in spite of that, and in spite of the
proverbial unhealthiness of the country, I am glad
and thankful to leave France—to leave the *Bagne.*

Perhaps I shall never see you again: perhaps I
shall see you some day when I am altered and grown
old with captivity and bad climate. If ever I have
the happiness of meeting you, dear Father, I shall
be able to speak of the fortress of Vanves and the
March of 1849 as of a dream—a terrible night-mare.
Now, Father, a thousand times adieu. Pray do not

forget me in your prayers. Ask for me of the great
and merciful God the strength I need to bear the
trials of the new position I have chosen with patience
and in a Christian spirit. Ask Him, too, to give me
moral courage to persevere in my good resolutions,
so as one day to share in the blessedness He has
promised. May God keep you, Father, and bless
your work ; and may He give a Christian peace to
poor distracted France.

Your son in Jesus Christ,

ANDRE CHOPART.

Kedu, Salut,

September 1, 1852.

My dear Father,—You must often have said to
yourself, 'Chopart is an ungrateful fellow ; he has
forgotten the friend who was so kind to him, who
prepared him so carefully to endure his terrible sentence as a Christian ought.' No, Father, I never
forgot you, but I busied myself too much with politics
at the *Bagne* to think about practising my religious
duties. You know better than I do what our Lord
said about not being able to serve two masters at
once—God and the world. I confess, in all sincerity,
that I preferred politics to God. But while confessing
my faults, dear Father, I must tell you that I never
had the ideas of the rest about priests : I have always
been a Catholic. . . . When I sailed for Guiana I
made a firm resolution to live a Christian life. In
France, at the *Bagne*, I chose to neglect performing my
religious duties, rather than perform them in dispositions
so unsuited to the dignity and sanctity of the acts. I

did wrong, I know; but I do think it would have been worse still to act like a hypocrite.

My dear Father, you have always shown a paternal interest in me : often you have condescended to devote some moments of your time to me. A letter from you has always been a joy and a comfort to me. So far away as I am from country, mother, and the few real friends who, in spite of my sentence, were faithful to me in trouble, I want some consolation. Will you, Father, forgive me for asking you to write to me now and then ?

I like being here far better than at the *Bagne.* Life is a shade less dreadful; and then, in a few months I hope to get a little position in Guiana, for I must tell you that this is a small island three leagues off the mainland. As I am so new to the place, I had better say nothing just yet as to my notions of it, bad or good. I will do so later on. And I will now end by begging you to remember me and pray for me.

Your son in Jesus Christ,

ANDRE CHOPART.

The Jesuit Fathers, who had nobly volunteered to be the chaplains of the poor *déportés*, bore witness to André's perseverance. One of them said that, once converted to God, he advanced rapidly in the path of resignation, penance, and humility.

My dearest Father [he wrote in June, 1856], God in His mercy and goodness always made me feel shame and remorse while I was living as those do who have no faith. My uneasy conscience always warned me

D

that eternal misery would be the punishment of so sinful a life. I can truly say, that if I kept my faith through it, it was a miracle of goodness due to the protection of our Blessed Lady and to the kind letters you so often wrote to me, and which I read and re-read even in my worst days. Since Easter I have been so happy as often to approach the altar. How I wish I could lead a life pure enough to be able to do so daily! My dear Father, I beg you of your charity to get some prayers for me after my death. I will take care that you shall hear of it. I have no one on whom I can depend for this service, and yet, when I think of all my sins, I may well say, as Bayard did, that if I could fast in a desert on bread and water for a thousand years, it would not be enough for their expiation. I ask this of you, Father, knowing that I shall not always be the one to see others die,[1] and that my turn will come. And I am not afraid of death. Not that I rely on any merits of my own, but only on God's great mercy.

Your most humble and respectful son in
Jesus Christ,

ANDRE CHOPART.

He did, in fact, die a very few years later, in the arms of the good Fathers who had done so much for him, and from whom M. de Ségur received the details of his holy death.

[1] He had just witnessed the deaths of two Jesuit Fathers within a fortnight of each other.

CHAPTER III.

Priest's work in Paris.

AMONG the most useful and admirable of the many useful and admirable *œuvres* of Paris are those of the young apprentices and of the *Cercles Catholiques*. We have all heard, some of us may have seen, something of the wonderful fruits of these great works, which have done more than any others, perhaps, for the Christianizing of the teeming world of the young artizan life of Paris. The "Patronages" of the first-mentioned *œuvre* are too many to enumerate, and there are four hundred "*Cercles*" now in active operation: may they be the leaven to keep from corruption the class exposed to socialistic and communistic influences, far more widely spread, and, we may venture to say, more depraved and dangerous, than those to counteract which these noble works were set on foot! But, like all great things, they had very small beginnings. "God's mills grind slowly," and it is of these early days that we must now speak.

The Patronages were first begun in 1845, but they were little known or thought of till the Revolu-

tion of 1848 rudely aroused the indifferent or infidel
bourgeoisie of Paris to the necessity of attending to
the working classes, who, neglected as they were,
became an easy prey to the socialists of the day.
Since the great Revolution there had been no single
legislative measure to protect the wretched children
of the people from the hideous abuses and miseries
prevalent in the workshop, and abetted or winked
at by wicked and selfish masters. The Society of
St. Vincent of Paul was not slow to discover these
evils in the course of its ministrations, and its members founded several Patronages for apprentices, but
without the active labours of a devoted priest the
amount of good done could be but small. The
Abbé de Ségur was one of the first to see the need,
and with him to see was to set to work to supply
it. He threw himself into the thing with all the
spirit and energy of his nature, and, to the last
moment of his life, this and kindred labours among
poor children, apprentices, and young workmen,
were above all others the objects of his predilection ;
it was his first and last vocation.

Up to this time priests and laymen, even the
holiest and most devoted, doubted, almost despaired,
of awakening the spiritual life in the children and
young workmen of Paris under the social and in-
dustrial conditions of their existence, such as it was.
Was the problem to be solved? The question was
discussed at the Patronage of the Rue du Regard,
the first that had been founded, and the Abbé de

Ségur was there to answer that it could. From the
very first he was on terms so friendly and intimate
with the children that everything came easy to him.
He was made for this new apostolate; he had every
gift, every quality for it. His brother's words are :
"To say the truth, paradoxical as the statement
may at first appear, there was something more than
sympathy: there was a positive resemblance between
the well-born young priest and the working lad of
Paris. There was the same frankness, the same
buoyancy, the quick perception, the familiar gaiety,
the ready wit, the word which calls up a laugh as
well as that which goes to the heart and draws
tears. They recognized and understood each other
at the first glance, with half a word." His power
over the children of the Patronage was so great,
and its good effects were so evident, that some of
the directors very soon conceived the idea of having
a Paschal Retreat. It was a bold notion for those
days; nothing of the kind had ever been attempted,
and not a few even of the most zealous of the
directors declared it to be utterly unpractical and
unreasonable, but as the Abbé de Ségur was ready
to give it, the thing was agreed to. A grain of
mustard seed, indeed! The retreat was not even
preached in a chapel—the Patronage had none—
but in one of the rooms of the house in the Rue du
Regard. A pious pupil of Pierre Olivaint's lent a
relic of the True Cross for the occasion, which was
placed on a bracket at the end of the room. The re-

treatants heard Mass at Saint-Sulpice, and received Benediction in the chapel of the Lazarist Fathers, but, humble as these beginnings were, they were crowned with success. The Apprentices' Paschal Retreat was regularly started, and henceforth it took place yearly. Then, as the houses became more numerous, a general retreat was given for them all. A few years more, and the work had so developed and increased that no church could contain the numbers who flocked to the general retreat, and the original plan of separate retreats for each Patronage again became the rule; but the survivors of this " day of small things " still speak with emotion and tenderness of that first retreat preached by the Abbé de Ségur to a handful of poor lads in the Rue du Regard.

The *œuvre* of the " Cercles Catholiques " was the natural development of the Patronages. The apprentices became young workmen, exposed to all the dangers of the workshop, all the temptations of Paris—dangers and temptations which grow with the growth of these lads, who, as experience had taught the Abbé de Ségur, if they *may* become so many apostles in the family, too often ruin the work of the patronage in the souls of its younger members. The question was, then, how to continue the influence of a work originally intended for children over youths emerging from apprenticeship, without sacrificing the interests of the former. The directors of the house in the Rue du Regard again gave M. de Ségur *carte blanche,* and again the result was a great success. The attics of the house were turned out, and "done up" as tastefully as means permitted, and all the youths over sixteen were invited to come on Sunday evenings. There were games and amusements of different kinds, and cakes and refreshing drinks were provided, but *the* attraction was the presence of the young Abbé, whose gaiety, kindness, and indescribable charm were the life and soul of these meetings, which were the germ and nucleus of the *Cercle Mont-Parnasse*, still the type and model of the four hundred others now existing. To the end of his life he retained an especial affection for it, and when, in 1880, the "silver wedding" of the *Cercle* was celebrated, he accepted with delight an invitation to honour this family gathering with his presence. He was already struck by the malady which was to be his last, and could not preside at the dinner in consequence, but as soon as it was over he came in and addressed a few words of exhortation to the assembly, among whom were some of the eldest-born of his apostolate.

It was not enough for his inexhaustible charity to give his time and thoughts and labours to his children : his home must be theirs too. His room in the Rue Cassette had a kind of little ante-chamber, which he devoted to them. The walls were hung with book-shelves, and the table was covered with sketches and engravings, among which were always a number of caricatures by Cham, whose rare merit it is to be almost invariably as unobjectionable as

he is talented. This room was always open to the
apprentices and school-boys of the neighbourhood,
and here they came to see their friend and father
and adviser, to chat with him freely, to be consoled
in every trouble and helped in every difficulty. It
seems that the Rue Cassette had hitherto enjoyed a
reputation for great quiet, not to say dulness, but
the good Abbé had completely revolutionized it   The
Paris *gamin*, even the most pious, is rather a noisy
creature, and the rush and clatter of feet, the shout-
ing and laughter which announced the presence of
the Abbé's visitors, excited much dissatisfaction and
some wonder as to what these young barbarians
wanted there. They were not long ignorant of the
name of the guilty party, for in their enthusiasm
the lads would sometimes dash along the street with
a shout of "Long live M. de Ségur!" When he
was appointed auditor of the Rota, and went to
Rome, the good folks of the Rue Cassette must
have enjoyed their return to peace and quietness all
the more from the force of contrast.

We will describe another favourite work of Gaston
de Ségur in the words of Mgr. de Conny, one of the
four priests with whom he lived in community.

He had begun the habit of questioning the miserable children who were sent to beg in the streets,
asking whether they attended any catechism class,
and whether they had made their First Communion.
The answer was too often a negative, and then he

offered to teach them and prepare them for this great
act of a Christian's life. Many accepted with sincere
eagerness, and their numbers increased so much that
it became necessary to organize the thing regularly,
and the Abbé de Ségur made an arrangement by
which one of the Christian Brothers of the house in
the Rue de Fleurus was charged with the individual
instruction of those children who were unable to
attend any school or catechism. In the evenings
Gaston de Ségur gave a little discourse to those
whom he found assembled, and was ready to hear
the confessions of all who wished it.

When a certain number were prepared there was
a First Communion, and all those who were present
were deeply touched by the piety with which the
children approached the altar. In the evening
they were the guests of their saintly catechist.
For my part, living as I did in community with
Gaston de Ségur, and being present at these happy
little festivals, I cannot say how I delighted in
them, how I wondered at the work wrought by the
holy lessons and the joys of religion in these souls,
which I should have thought blighted by their
miserable antecedents. How happy they were, poor
things, to feel themselves treated with kindness and
respect, and how anxious to continue to deserve
this treatment! I know that I never shared in any
festivity which was like those little suppers to me.
Let me add that the good resolutions of these
children were not transient. I knew enough of my
friend's good works to be able to state, either on

my own testimony or on that of others on whom I can depend, that their firmness was often very remarkable.

Besides the four important works of which we have given a slight sketch, the military prisons, the Patronages, the young workmen's *Cercles*, and the Catechisms of the Rue de Fleurus; there was the Confraternity of the Holy Family in the Rue de Sèvres, composed of the poor of both sexes, to whom he preached a discourse on Sundays after the Mass; a distribution of alms, according to the needs of each member, concluding the meetings. He worked so hard and so incessantly that his doctor assured him that if he intended to kill himself, he had only to continue for six months longer as he was doing. In fact, not . more than a year after his ordination, he was obliged to suspend all active work for a time, and was not even allowed to say Mass for several weeks. A season at Eaux-Bonnes, and a short visit to Les Nouettes, restored his health, and he returned with increased energy and delight to his beloved "floating parish" of prisoners, workmen, and destitute children.

At this period of the biography the Marquis de Ségur gives the Rule of life which his brother laid down for himself on leaving the Seminary, to shew that it was from a spirit of truly apostolic zeal, and not from any imprudent recklessness that in so

short time he had over-taxed his strength. It is
preceded by this :

EXAMEN OF CONSCIENCE.

Have I lived to-day as a Christian, that is, as a
man who is to live throughout eternity, conformed to
Christ, and dead to myself, the world and sin ?

Have I shrunk from sharing my Master's Cross,
His *humility*, His love of humiliation, abjection and
neglect ? His Hidden Life ; His *sweetness and patience*
in regard to God, my neighbour and myself? His
interior and exterior *mortification* in my thoughts,
imaginations, words, actions, looks and the rest of
my senses ? His *poverty*, by living detached from all
things in this world and directing all my aims and
efforts to life eternal in Jesus Christ ? His *purity*,
avoiding every occasion of sin and every freedom ?
His *obedience*, seeking in all things the Will of God
only ? His *piety* towards His Father, in all my
actions, especially in the works of the sacred ministry ?
His spirit of *sacrifice* and oblation, regarding myself as
a victim of religion to God in union with Jesus Christ,
and of sanctification for the world ?

Am I conformed to Christ in my *understanding*, my
thoughts, instructions, comparisons, judgments ? in my
heart, its affections, antipathies, inclinations, in my
words, in my whole behaviour ?

Have I lived as a priest, that is, as a saint and
sanctifier of others ? Have I sought the glory of my
Divine Master all day ? Have I done all that He
expected of me for the salvation of the souls He died
for on Calvary ?

RULE OF LIFE.

The Christian and sacerdotal spirit is the soul of my life. *Exercises of piety and ministrations* are its body.

Evening Examen: To think of my meditation and prepare it carefully.

Retire to rest punctually, before ten o'clock, with recollection, penitence and modesty.

During the night, lift up my heart to Jesus and Mary. Rise punctually—great promptitude and generosity.

Mental prayer, the soul of my day and of my sacerdotal life—seek in it above all things union with Jesus Christ and contempt of myself. An hour, unless necessarily hindered. Before beginning, a fervent renewal of my devotions and consecration to the Blessed Virgin.

Spirit of prayer during the day—actual union with our Lord.

Office—as nearly as possible at canonical hours. Great spirit of religion and affection of heart—if possible, on my knees.

Holy Mass. Great care in immediate preparation—general and particular intentions, annihilation before the Divine Majesty.

At the Altar, deep devotion, losing myself in our Lord Jesus Christ. Rubrics.

Silence before and after. Thanksgiving, twenty minutes, affection and attention to the Presence of Jesus Christ. " *Manete in Me et Ego in vobis.*"

Sacred Scripture, the science of the priest—daily, especially the Holy Gospel in order the better to know our Lord Jesus Christ, Who is Life Eternal.

Study—in a spirit of faith and prayer. Regular work. Not to let myself be absorbed by the duties of my sacred ministry. Prepare my instructions well —mistrust of my own facility. No *loitering* in my room.

Entire devotion to Our Lady. To act in a spirit of dependence on the Mother of God, for *everything* in me belongs to her. Ask her blessing on going out and coming in. Meditate during Rosary.

Conversation—" *Qui non offendit verbo, hic perfectus est vir.*" Judge no one, least of all my superiors and brother-priests. Avoid detraction, quizzing. Speech reserved, prudent, simple, gentle and modest. Nothing about confessions or politics. Nothing frivolous.

Manners amiable, peaceable and grave, I should see Jesus Christ in my brethren : " *Mihi fecistis.*"

Meals—religion, simplicity, mortification, reasonable care of my health. Not to pay attention to the dishes.

Monthly Retreat with my brother-priests.

Confession. Weekly, at least.

Indulgences. Gain as many as possible, and give them to Our Lady, the absolute mistress of all my spiritual and temporal goods.

Regulation of expenses. Buy nothing superfluous for myself. No bills, unless unavoidable.

Preaching—simple, solid, useful, well prepared, suitable to the Word of God and the dignity of the priesthood, like the Preaching of our Lord, my Pattern in all things.

Sacrament of Penance—devote myself wholly to it, especially to the confessions of poor children. Spirit of faith, charity and prudence—to see and love them in our Lord Jesus Christ only: " *Quamdiu fecistis uni ex his fratribus Meis minimis, Mihi fecistis.*"

A single soul cost the Life and Passion of God our Saviour : " *Bonus pastor animam suam dat pro ovibus suis.*"

It had been for some time in contemplation to compile a manual of devotion for the use of the members of the Patronages, and one of the directors of that in the Rue du Regard thought of adding to this manual a little pamphlet entitled, " Answers to the principal objections against religion." He decided, however, that neither the objections nor the answers met the case ; and knowing that the Abbé de Ségur was under orders to give up all work involving the use of his voice, he felt sure that he should be conferring rather than incurring an obligation by proposing that he should do some work for God by his pen during this period of enforced activity. The result was the little book of *Réponses* which, somewhat developed and enlarged at a later period, has had so great a success and done so great a work for souls innumerable, having passed, in thirty years, through several hundred editions and been translated into almost every European, and even into the Hindu language.

At first the little book seemed likely to come to nothing. The Society of St. Vincent had begun to publish and distribute good books, and the president of one of the Conferences proposed the publication of the *Réponses* to the Council.   One of the body, a distinguished literary man, who afterwards became a member of the French Academy, was commissioned to examine the Abbé de Ségur's book and report upon it. He did so, and while acknowledging the good intention of the author, he decided that it had no other merit, that it was like a score of others which unfortunately go far to justify the opinion that all good books are very dull reading.   Well ! it was a blow certainly ; but Gaston de Ségur made spiritual capital out of the humiliation, as he did out of everything that befel him ; he offered it to God and thought no more of the matter ; but his friends were not disposed to take things so quietly, and never doubted that a good Catholic publisher would be found to undertake the business.   This again proved a failure.   It was then proposed to him to publish on his own account, but this he refused to do ; his humility acquiesced in the judgment passed by high authority on the book, and he said simply that his money belonged to the poor, and his conscience forbade his employing it in this way.

The poor manuscript therefore was put away, and so effectually, that when Madame de Ségur expressed a wish to read it, it was nowhere to be found, and was only discovered by chance in looking for something else by a servant who took it to her. A year before, a two hundred franc note had been found on the staircase of her house, and after setting the police to work and trying all ways to find out the owner in vain, she had come to the conclusion that she was at liberty to use it for a charitable object. Now it seemed to the good mother that she could not apply it to a better purpose than that of publishing Gaston's little book, and so at length it saw the light. It is no wonder, when we consider the good it has done and the failure with which it was threatened, that the Marquis de Ségur should see in all this the Hand of God trying the author's humility and marking with the sign of the Cross his first effort in a line in which he was to do so much for His Son and for the souls so dear to Him. Accustomed as he was to see the action of Providence in everything, he took the success of his first attempt as a sign that God would have him serve Him by his pen as well as by the active works of his ministry.

Not long after this, another opportunity presented itself. The Society of St. Vincent had begun the practice of distributing little tracts or leaflets, which each visitor gave together with the weekly dole for food, reading and explaining them first when necessary. This was the origin of the *Little Readings* with which the name of Mgr. de Ségur is so closely associated. It was a work after his own heart, one for which he had all the necessary gifts, and he threw himself into it with a zeal which never relaxed even when occupied in important and absorbing functions in Rome. He writes, in July, 1852, to one of the members of the Council of the Society: "I

am just sending off some articles for the *Little
Readings* to M. Baudon; he is perfectly free to make
any corrections he likes as to manner, but not as to
matter, for in respect of doctrine a word more or
less may make heresy of what is said. , . , I particularly wish you not to allow your good and over-
scrupulous colleagues to soften down my phrases.
That is taking the salt out of the soup. I consider
the important article on ' Blasphemy' a failure just
because of these corrections : you can no longer tell
that it treats of the coarse blasphemy which is so
universal. The chief merit of my little articles is
that I dot my *i*'s and go straight to the point, taking
my readers for what they are—extremely ignorant.
One reason why sermons are sometimes so dull is
that priests affect a conventional style, beating
about the bush, and trying to say something new."

The Abbé de Ségur was assiduous in visiting all
his spiritual children and all his poor friends who
were in the hospitals, where he was always at the
disposal of the Sisters of Charity or any pious
persons who might beg him to console or convert
some particular patient. A young needlewoman
who was in the habit of visiting the Hôpital Baujon,
one of those holy souls of whom there are so many
of her class in Paris, spoke to him once of a young
Swede dying there of consumption whom she had
been doing her best to help for some time. He was
an artist who had come to Paris full of hopes which
had ended in disappointment and broken health :
E

he was utterly alone, and welcomed the charitable
visits of this good girl as those of an angel of
consolation. "How is it possible," he asked, "that
you can care as you do for a stranger?" His gratitude gave her courage to speak of prayer, and for
her sake, he consented to wear a miraculous medal
and to recite the *Mémorare*, but he would only agree
to see a priest on condition that he should not
speak to him about religion. In this way the Abbé
de Ségur made poor Gabriel Edmann's acquaint-
ance. In the first interview, faithful to his promise,
he confined himself to kind and affectionate expressions of interest; but the young man's heart
was won at once, as all simple hearts were, by the
unspeakable charm of his nature and manner, and
the second time he came there were no prejudices
to overcome, the young artist's soul and the priest's
were in communication, and the task was henceforth
an easy one. Gabriel cried like a child as he listened
to the simple, fervent words in which his new friend
spoke to him of Jesus and Mary, of the sacraments
and of Heaven. "No one ever spoke to me like that,"
he said. The Abbé spent several hours in instructing
him, then, having learnt from the Sister that the end
was near, and finding him in excellent dispositions,
resolved to receive his abjuration without delay. It
was the 30th of November, and the Abbé gave him,
in baptizing him, the name of Andrew in addition to
his own. "What a happiness!" he said, "it is a feast-
day indeed for me. Thank God for bringing me here."

Gabriel died the next day.   Here is an extract from a letter in which the young workwoman, who brought M. de Ségur to poor Gabriel's bedside, describes the impression made on him by his visitor: "The Sunday after M. de Ségur's visit, the poor young man caught my hand the moment he saw me, saying, 'But, my good sister' (he used to call me so), 'it is an angel not a man that you sent to see me!   One cannot look at that young priest without seeing God in him.'   He could talk of nothing but M. de Ségur, how he might have such a fine position and had given it all up to be a priest and to serve God better. . . . 'If it were God's will that I should get well, the first time I went out should be to hear his Mass and have Holy Communion from him.   I would obey him in everything.'"   Must we not say, as his brother does, "happy the priest whose soul is so penetrated and radiant with the Divine Spirit, as to merit and justify this sublime testimony of the penitent sinner, the converted Protestant?"   One cannot look at him without seeing God in him!   It is like the definition of an apostle given by St. Paul: "I live, now not I, but Christ liveth in me."

To all these various works of corporal and spiritual mercy the Abbé de Ségur added what his brother calls his "family ministrations," a work which went on increasing during his whole life. He made it a duty to celebrate the marriages of his relations, to baptize their children, to prepare them

for first Communion and Confirmation, to console
them in sickness or sorrow, to assist them in their
last moments, and to commit their bodies to the
grave.   His affectionate and earnest exhortations
so wrought upon his great-grandmother, Madame
d'Aguesseau, who had lived for more than fifty
years in heresy, that she consented, at the age of
eighty, to see Père de Ravignan, who received her
abjuration, and the closing years of her long life
were spent in prayer and penance.

We cannot resist quoting this beautiful letter from
Mgr. de Ségur to his brother, the future Marquis,
on the occasion of his marriage.

What shall I say to you, my dear brother, on this
happy day so anxiously desired?   You know my affection for you; the natural bond between us has been
strengthened by the sacred bond of grace, and I have
ong loved in you not a brother only, but a friend of
the Lord, Who is my Life and my All.

You and I are the eldest sons of the house; we are
called to be its heads.   I was to have been the head
before men, but I chose the better part, to be the head
before God, and you have supplied my place in the
post which I have left for a higher vocation.   As priest
and head of our family, I am answerable for its honour
before God; as man of the world and head of the
same family, you will be answerable for its honour
before men.   Every day, in the glorious ministry of
the altar, I offer this family, in its present no less than
ts past and future generations, to God, praying our

Divine Lord to give them a share in His Redemption and eternal glory, apart from which all glory is a dream and a chimera; while you, who are called to duties less sublime, but not less necessary, must study to continue worthy of your fathers and to become one day a pattern to your children.

Now the secret of honour, both before men and before God, is all told in one word—to be a true Christian. That includes everything, the performance of the great duties of life, whether public or private; justice, integrity, energy, and perseverance, as well as the equally important qualities of kindness, gentleness, and forbearance. It is also the secret of happiness—for happiness is involved in duty, like the fruit in the shell. . . . Always united in Him Who is the Supreme Peace, Goodness, Mercy, Truth, and Life, your affection will draw from the fountain of the love of Christ a strength and a sweetness ever new, and the marriage-tie will make you better instead of alluring you from God, as it does sometimes. . . . What I particularly wish to remind you of on this solemn day is the power which holy almsgiving possesses of paralysing the dangers of riches and sanctifying a high position. Give alms, love the poor, help them, assist them, seek them out. Go into their dwellings to dry their tears, to feed the hungry, to clothe the naked, and to make those that are desolate feel that they have still friends, brothers, and servants on earth. Give to them largely and joyously, and when you have given, give again and give continually. Never did almsgiving impoverish or ruin any one. Do not listen to the voice of human prudence, but show that it is possible for a Christian to unite the lowly works of charity with the more brilliant ones of a higher social position. . . . In conclusion, my brother and sister, I ask our Blessed Lady to obtain God's blessing for you. Like the bride and bridegroom of Cana, you have invited her and her Son to your wedding. From the bottom of your hearts you will listen to her when she says to you, as she said to that blessed pair, ' Whatsoever He shall say to you, do it.' Your fidelity to Mary's words will be the pledge of your happiness both in this life and in the changeless rest of eternity. May we all attain to it by the mercy of God and the merits of our Lord Jesus Christ !

CHAPTER IV.

In Rome.

THE year 1852 brought great changes to France, involving a great change in Mgr. de Ségur's life. It will be well to say a few words of his view of the *coup d'état.* It was, of course, before all things, a Christian view; for in politics, as in everything, he looked only to the glory of God and the good of souls; and in common with the immense majority of the clergy and the Christian laity, he hailed with relief and satisfaction the advent of a strong Government prepared to put down anarchy and confusion. There can be little doubt that but for the election of Louis Napoleon, the Legislative Assembly of 1851 would have ended in becoming what the National Assembly did become twenty years later.

When the invasion of the Papal States in 1860 so fatally annihilated the confidence of Catholics and the hopes they had cherished of Louis Napoleon, Mgr. de Ségur sadly said his *meâ culpâ* on the subject to the illustrious Bishop of Poitiers, who made answer that France so greatly needed a Charlemagne in 1852 that she might well be excused for being determined to see a Charlemagne in the Prince.

Events did indeed prove the fallacy of her expectations, but, to say the least, the evil day was put off
for twenty years, during which Catholic institutions
prospered and increased. As the Marquis de Ségur
says: "We may judge of their progress by
their ruins; and before condemning those who,
without inviting the *coup d'état*, without even justify-
ing either its principle or manner of execution,
accepted its consequences with prompt resignation
and legitimate hopes, one should be able to foresee
what would have been the result of the regular course
of events, the maintenance of the Constitution of
1848, and of the General Election fixed for May,
1852." The Abbé de Ségur accepted the new
Government with no other political idea than
St. Paul's *desideratum* for the Church and her children, "to lead a quiet and peaceable life."

His own peace and quiet were now to be broken in
upon in a way for which he was little prepared.
One of the first objects which engaged the attention
of the new ruler of France was her relations with
the Holy See, and immediately after his accession
to power he made known his intention to send to
Rome an "Auditor of the Rota" for France, with
an especial view to the revision of the notorious
"organic articles" which, while professing to carry
out the Concordat, were in reality its practical con-
tradiction. The Prince also expressed a strong
desire for the modification of the laws regarding
civil marriage, education, and other important

subjects, so as to bring them into harmony with the decrees of the Council of Trent. Of course the proposal was eagerly accepted by the Holy Father, and the French Government at once addressed itself to the task—no easy one—of finding the right man for the post. It was by what people call an "accident" that M. Turgot, the Minister for Public Affairs, mentioned the name of M. de Ségur to the President. He was an old friend of the Comte de Ségur, and had heard the highest character of his son in the days when the latter was a young *attaché* in Rome. The Prince consented to see the Abbé, who was strongly urged by his father to accept the appointment, should it be offered to him.

It was a thunderbolt to Gaston, carrying destruction to all his ideas of the vocation and labours for which God had marked him out : he believed himself entirely devoid of aptitude for judicial or political business, and his first impulse was to give an unqualified refusal to the overtures made to him. But, in the true spirit of faith and humility, he resolved not to take upon himself the entire responsibility of so important a decision. He took time for consideration, above all for prayer, he consulted wise and holy men to whom he submitted the question ; and the voice of conscience thus enlightened was not the same as that of his inclination. His aversion for dignities proved them to be the less dangerous to him ; if he sorrowed over leaving the simple souls he loved so well, he must consider

the services it would be in his power to render to a
whole nation by his influence; and so, in a spirit of
duty and sacrifice, he yielded, not knowing that He
Who accepted that sacrifice would recompense it
even in this world, by bringing him back to his
lowly apostolate, after some years of useful labour
in Rome, sanctified by the immense blessings and
privileges of the holy city, by close and affectionate
intimacy with the Father of the faithful, and above
all by the life-long cross whose first touch he was so
soon to feel.

His first audience with the President was decisive;
M. de Ségur was charmed with the graceful kindness, too simple and spontaneous to be called
affability, which every one felt who was admitted
to confidential communication with Louis-Napoleon;
while the latter, who was, as the Marquis de Ségur
remarks, as simple and amiable in private life as he
was selfish and wily in politics, was equally pleased
with the Abbé. Here was a man with no ambition
but that of serving God, who earnestly desired
cordial relations between France and the Holy See,
who would go straight to the point without any
alarms as to how far he might be personally com-
promised, and who would be sure to tell him the
truth. He spoke very frankly of the irregularities
of his youth, of his old prejudices against the
Papal Government, declaring that experience had
opened his eyes, and that he earnestly desired that
peace and harmony with Rome which he believed

to be as necessary for the State as for the Church. To the day of his death Mgr. de Ségur believed that *then*, at least, he was sincere.

So the little community in the Rue Cassette was breaking up : two of its members, the Abbé de Conny and the Abbé Gibert, having gone to Moulins, the former as Vicar-General, the latter as Canon. Here is an extract from a letter from M. de Conny to Gaston de Ségur and the three others still in the old house :

What is the spell, my good friends, that has been cast over our poor community? It is being broken up bit by bit ; in order, no doubt, to put the different pieces in a very grand setting ; but anyhow, it is coming to an end in the making of canons, vicars-general, and auditors of the Rota. I do not know what the rest of our brethren are to become ; to be set on some pinnacle or other, I dare say, but I can assure you I am quite sad at the thought of your being all scattered. Brother Gaston, do not be long in paying me your visit. . . , You must go, like Jephte's daughter, who went to bewail her virginity among her companions, to lament your obscurity, your littleness, which you are going to be robbed of in order to be made a personage, for good and all. Your sacrifice is made ; I know there is no going back, but I feel sure you will find it hard work to be taking everywhere about with you a man of importance, and not to be able to come and go, speak and act simply without fuss. I know *I* find it hard to resign myself to all these inconvenient dignities in your case.

To this letter the Abbé Gibert added a neat
Latin postscript, which loses a good deal in the
translation :

" Alas ! Brother Gaston, ' how is the finest colour
changed ! ' From black you have become purple,
from a subject a superior, from children's confessor
auditor. I condole with you instead of congratu-
lating you. Why did not I stay with you ? Why
did not you stay with us ? At all events may our
Lord Jesus stay with us, for it is towards evening—
Farewell ! "

As to Gaston de Ségur's innumerable " parish-
ioners," the poor Paris *gamins*, artisans, and soldiers,
their consternation may be imagined. It seemed to
them like parting for ever, in spite of his assurances
of constant prayers and affection, his promises to
spend his three months' vacation among them every
year. To the most devoted he promised to write,
and the promise was faithfully kept. The following
touching little letter is from a young workman, to
whom Mgr. de Ségur was much attached, and to
whom he had given hopes of taking him some day
into his service.

Dear M. l'Abbé,—I take the liberty of writing you
a line, as I have not had time to come to take leave of
you. I am so glad I have your likeness, for whenever
I am tempted to go wrong, I shall only have to look
at it to bring you before me. I thank you a thousand
times for all your goodness to me and my mother.
You don't know what a grief your going away is to

me : it makes such a blank—I cannot describe it. My
comfort is that I hope our good God will bring us
together again some day, it is what I ask Him for
every day, night and morning. What happiness it
would be to be near you—in your house! If that
came about, I should feel safe for eternity. I promise
you to go often to Confession, and to receive Holy
Communion every month, for remember I am going to
be with a lot of bad characters, and to hear bad
words and swearing all day. Then, if I get out of
work, how shall I manage to help my poor mother
and to keep myself? I shall not have you like a good
father, near me—oh! I can never say how good you
were to me. Do, pray, send me a bit of an answer.
I shall often write to you, and you will give me good
advice like a father. Now I must end and say goodbye, and embrace you with all my heart. I wish you
a good voyage without any accident. A whole year
before I shall see you again, my kind friend and
father! I am for life your humble, obedient, faithful
friend,

ERNEST S.

Early in the May of 1852, then, M. de Ségur left
France ; his mother promised to join him in Rome
for the winter with her daughters, for one of whom,
Sabine, "the saint of the family," this visit was the
prelude and, as it were, consecration of the offering
of herself which she was about to make to God in
the Convent of the Visitation.

The four years spent by Mgr. de Ségur in Rome
may be considered as the second portion of his life,

to be succeeded by twenty-five years of an apostolate still more extensive and vigorous than that which preceded his appointment to the functions of Auditor of the Rota. As it is to this apostolic work that this sketch is chiefly devoted, we shall pass as quickly as possible over these four years, but the portrait would be unfinished without some notice of them ; and, as will be seen, he was both ingenious and successful in devising ways and means for combining the labours dearest to his heart with the exercise of the new functions, in which he did good service for God and His Church.

Pius the Ninth was eagerly expecting the young Auditor, and no sooner had the latter arrived at the Vatican, where his cousin, Mgr. de Mérode, resided as Chaplain to the Pope, than he was summoned to the presence of His Holiness, before whom he had to appear, just as he was, all covered with the dust of his journey. The Holy Father embraced him affectionately, and during the whole of his residence in Rome he admitted him to the closest intimacy, and bestowed on him a thousand marks of the tenderest regard. The two most intimate friends of Mgr. de Ségur at Rome were Mgr. de Mérode and Mgr. Bastide, of whom the Marquis gives an interesting sketch. The former, as is well known, was a soldier before he was a priest, and a soldier he remained all his life. Louis Veuillot said of him, that he was made of the same stuff as Julius the Second, and Augustin Cochin described him as a sword sheathed in a cassock. Full of humility and burning charity, he was, however, not only terrible to the enemies of God and the Church, but rather alarming, at times, to those he most loved and respected : he would contradict the Pope himself, who liked him none the less for his freedom. His austerity of life was extreme. Certainly Mgr. de Ségur was not in the habit of treating his body too tenderly, but he said laughingly of the few days he spent with his cousin on first coming to Rome, that he had never been so much edified nor so ill fed in his life.

Monseigneur, or, as he was at this time, the Abbé Bastide, had passed his youth in the gayest circles of Paris. Suddenly, in the midst of his career of pleasure, he was overcome by a feeling of disgust for its emptiness, and went straight to the Roman College. His vocation as military chaplain was made plain during the siege of Rome, when he joined Mgr. de Mérode in rendering the most devoted attentions to the French soldiers, and during the twenty years of the occupation of the city by the French army he was its chaplain, friend and father. His enthusiasm for Rome was a passion, and he had no greater pleasure than that of acting as guide to pilgrims of every grade, from his beloved troopers to the most distinguished statesmen. Such were the men who were for a time to be to Gaston de Ségur what Mgr. Gay and the other brethren of the Rue Cassette had been in Paris.

No sooner was he initiated into his new duties, than he cast about how to help the Abbé Bastide with his huge military flock; he knew, indeed, that he had come to Rome on purpose to serve God in quite another way, but the longing for souls was too intense to allow him altogether to abandon the apostolate which was his very life. " I am greatly afraid," he writes to a friend, " that I shall not be able to hear the confessions of these dear fellows. One has to observe a certain etiquette with regard to the Court to which I belong. If I were to throw myself too openly into works of active charity, the tribunal of the Rota would be blamed for the loss of suits, and not only I should be complained of, but the Pope for choosing missionaries as judges. So I must do what I can without seeming to do anything." In this spirit of prudence he began by simply helping M. Bastide by preaching to the soldiers on Sundays, and by joining them in a large room appropriated to the purpose, where conversation, games, sermons disguised as stories, everything, in short, was utilized to bring God near to these souls, very good and simple ones as a rule, in which the piety of early days only needed the touch of a wise and tender hand to wake up into life and activity. He won their hearts readily, as usual ; and not being able to hear their confessions, he quietly prepared them and handed them over to the Abbé Bastide. This was the rule, at least; but the exceptions soon became tolerably numerous, and the

Auditor of the Rota was so often turned into confessor and director, that by and by the exception became the rule. These military *soirées* developed a good number of vocations, and who shall say how many souls were brought back to God by the Abbé Bastide and his unaccredited coadjutor? We will let one of these good French soldiers speak for himself :

Monseigneur,—You must forgive me for taking the liberty of writing these lines. I want you to know how heartily grateful I and a great many other soldiers are for the happiness you have given us. When first I wore the uniform, I said to myself, ' Now, my good parents, goodbye; I shall no longer have you to speak to me kindly and show me the importance of serving God.' I thought that, for a soldier, there was no more faith or religion, or kind charitable friends ; and indeed the first two months I was in garrison at Marseilles I only met with young soldiers who used disgraceful language and bragged of their vices. I used to pray to God to get me a change of post ; and there—in a few months I got it, for I was in Rome, where I found no more of that freedom of speech and bad talk : the reason was that the good fellows here had had the luck to hear your advice and profit by it. That was not all my good fortune—I heard you for the first time ! I could not help crying for joy as I heard your kind words. It is as though God had placed you among us as the father of us all. . . I never find the time long now—everything seems to go right. What a change it is ! I used to hate the

F

military profession, and now I thank God for putting
me in it.   There is Mgr. Bastide, too: there is no
saying how fond we all are of him.   It is to you and
him that I owe my happiness here.   Forgive me for
speaking in this way to you, but I am too full of
gratitude to be silent.   You speak so kindly to us, and
it is such a pleasure to a soldier to be talked to about
his family and his country.

To this humble tribute we will add one of a different kind, which gives a life-like picture of Mgr.
de Ségur's life in Rome.   The following extracts are
from an account written by the Abbé Klingenhoffen,
a Protestant officer in a regiment of Chasseurs,
when first Gaston de Ségur came to Rome, who
was converted by him and Mgr. Bastide, became a
priest, and acted as Mgr. de Ségur's secretary
during the last two years of his office.

The first time I saw Mgr. de Ségur was on the
occasion of some great feast, I think it was the beatifi-
cation of Blessed Germaine Cousin.   There was a
sudden block which stopped the carriages returning
from the function, and in one of these was a dignitary
whose striking appearance attracted my attention, and
who, to my surprise, saluted me courteously in return
for my fixed gaze.   I learned afterwards that it was
Mgr. de Ségur, a great friend of the French soldiers,
which explained the kind smile with which he had
greeted a stranger.   Some months later I fell sick,
and so made aquaintance with the Abbé Bastide, who
sent me Mgr. de Ségur's *Réponses*, and, when I was

recovering, introduced me to the author. He made me promise to visit him, lent me books, and was kind enough to instruct me himself. . . . He received my abjuration just before he left for France for the vacation during which he completely lost his sight. On his return, he asked me to be his secretary. . . . My vocation to the priesthood had been prophesied to me already by Pius the Ninth on my reception into the Church, and I entered Holy Orders the day of the proclamation of the dogma of the Immaculate Conception. There was quite a little congregation of us at the Palazzo Brancadoro, the youngest was the Abbé Jules Hugo, nephew to the poet. . . . He died the death of a saint soon after. A little later a brother of Mgr. de Ségur, who was Chief Secretary to the Embassy, joined us. In the morning we had prayers together, then we heard Mass ; work or study till eleven, reading and answering letters. After breakfast there were always numbers of visitors ; every Frenchman of note came to Mgr. de Ségur, who was always kind and charming, and inexhaustible in his advice on the way to see Rome well. In the afternoon we went out. . . . Mgr. de Ségur spent a long time in the evening in his chapel. . . . It was his time for hearing confessions, and every day brought some new penitents, among whom were many officers and soldiers. Kind and affable to everyone, he was especially so to the French. He had given strict orders that priests were not to be allowed to wait, but to be admitted, no matter what the time might be. One day, however —we were coming in very late—I saw in the ante-room an old priest, shabbily dressed, who had every appearance of coming to ask alms. Monseigneur was tired, and the servants thought it best not to announce his visitor till after supper ; so that the poor priest waited in silent patience for some time. After a while he said that he wished to go to confession, and was taken to the chapel, where, after supper, Monseigneur joined him. I heard him pouring forth apologies on leaving it. The visitor was the saintly Mgr. Villecourt, Bishop of Rochelle, on his way to the Vatican to be made Cardinal. When he paid his next visit, in state, to Mgr. de Ségur, it was amusing to see the embarrassed air of the servants as they went to receive him, at the bottom of the staircase, carrying tall wax candles, as is the etiquette before a Cardinal.

After supper the *salon* was open, and M. Klingenhoffen goes on to describe many of the *habitués*, among whom was the admirable General de Sabran-Pontevés, of whom his intimate friend, Colonel de Malherbe, said that he was sure he had never lost his baptismal innocence. He fell in the Crimean War. These evenings were delightful ; every one was at his ease, and so at his best, and the host as much the life and soul of this polished circle as he had been with his dear noisy guests in the Rue Cassette.

There were exceptions to this routine [M. Klingen-hoffen continues]. After Mass on Sundays there was a visit to the house of the Christian Brothers near the

Fountain of Trevi, which was especially devoted to the children of French soldiers, and which became a model of good conduct and piety. He gave the children an instruction, and catechized them, the good marks being rewarded by a distribution of cakes, the size of which was regulated by the marks, but it was whispered that Monseigneur was apt to strain a point so as to entitle a doubtful candidate to the highest ' very well,' and its corresponding cake of three sous.

Some of the children were, at first, very ill instructed, and these were the objects of his particular care. Through them he reached the parents, and gained them, too, to God. Souls were converted, wants relieved, marriages made between persons who had lived for years in unlawful unions. Every one trusted, no one feared him. He was repulsed by no difficulty, or rather, he refused to admit the existence of one when it was a question of God's glory and the salvation of souls. His ' I will see to it,' was like the famous *J'y penserai* of the Curé d'Ars.

When the illustrious Bishop of Poitiers visited the school of Trevi, Mgr. de Ségur presented to him two of his best boys, Léon Kämpf and Claude Rey, begging that they might be admitted into his Little Seminary at Montmorillon. The request was granted, and the lads set off alone, with a scanty purse and their letter of recommendation, and knocked one fine morning at the door of the Seminary. "Who sent you here?" "Mgr. de Ségur." "Where do you come from?" "From Rome."

They were received, and both did credit to their recommendations. Claude Rey died a holy death a few days after his ordination to the priesthood. His companion returned to Rome, and after earning his stripes as sergeant-major in fighting against the Garibaldians, finished his ecclesiastical studies, and is now curé of a parish in the diocese of Poitiers.

During the long beautiful days of the Roman summer and autumn of 1852, Mgr. de Ségur devoted much of his leisure to his favourite art. He wished to paint eight pictures of saints as illustrating the beatitudes, and several competent judges have pronounced his best work to be the figure of St. Ignatius, whom he chose for the last. He had just begun that of St. Charles, as the pattern of those who hunger and thirst after justice, when the loss of one of his eyes (in May, 1853) obliged him to lay down his pencil never to take it up again.

CHAPTER V.

The Vatican, the Tuileries, and Saint-Sulpice.

EVENTS were thickening in France. The President of the Republic was Emperor of the French. His marriage followed almost immediately, and he wrote soon after to the Holy Father expressing the great desire he had to be crowned by him. The letter was sent under cover to Mgr. de Ségur, to whom he also wrote in the same sense, adding some remarks on the burning question of the Organic Articles, which he admitted to be detrimental to religion as they stood, although he considered that to press their revision would be impolitic just then, as it would be regarded in the light of a concession to the Papal Court in return for the Pope's consent to crown him. Mgr. de Ségur went at once to the Vatican, where he was admitted to a private audience, the details of which were a secret for many years, and told to the Marquis long after by his brother. His account is very graphic and interesting. Mgr. de Ségur, kneeling at the feet of the Holy Father, presented the Emperor's letter to him. He read it half aloud with evident satisfaction, and when he had finished, said admiringly,

"This is a magnificent letter!" and went on to speak of the wish it expressed to be crowned by himself. "That is very natural," replied the young *Monsignore*, whom the Pope always encouraged to treat him with respectful familiarity; "if your Holiness were in his place, would you not do the same?" "No doubt—but there are difficulties." "Perhaps," Mgr. de Ségur ventured to say, "the idea would not be well received by some members of the Sacred College?" "No, no, the difficulties have nothing to do with the Cardinals; the thing is that an excellent Concordat is about to be made with Austria, and what would Austria say if I went to France? There would be a risk of breaking off the negociations. Besides," he went on in a tone grave to severity, "I cannot set foot in France so long as the Organic Articles exist. The first of them is a blow on my face" *(è un schiaffo per me.)* Then, after reading over again some passages of the letter—"Well, and what does Mgr. de Ségur think about it?"

The young auditor required some pressing before he spoke. At last he said: "Since your Holiness commands me to speak, this is what I think would be not only possible, but beneficial to the Church. It would prevent any discontent on the part of Austria if, after crowning the Emperor Napoleon at Paris, your Holiness were to go to Vienna to crown the Emperor of Austria. I think it would have a marvellous effect. No sooner would your

Holiness arrive in France than the nation would be
at your feet; it would be the death-blow to Gallicanism, and, once at Paris, the Emperor would
consent to everything you wish. From Paris your
Holiness would pass through Germany, and that
would be a decisive stroke against Protestantism,
which is incapable of satisfying the people, some of
whom are tending to infidelity, others to Catholicism.
It would be altogether such a triumph as the Holy
See has not had for many a day." The Pope listened in well-pleased silence, and replied, "*Ebbene,
andremo!* Well, then, we will go; only, if the
Emperor wishes me to do so, he must open the door.
Let him make a fresh Concordat much like the first,
of which the last article shall simply run thus:
'Every law or decree contrary to the present Con-
vention is hereby abrogated.' Then I will let three
months pass, that the Emperor may escape the
reproach he fears of having made a bargain for the
sake of gratifying his personal ambition, and then—
in carrozza!" Mgr. de Ségur wrote at once to
Napoleon in the plainest terms, and some weeks
later started for Paris, where he had a very cordial
interview with him, in the course of which he asked
the Emperor why he should not follow the example
of Charlemagne in going to be crowned at St. Peter's,
rather than that of Napoleon the First in being
crowned at Notre Dame. The Emperor answered
with a smile that he had no objection to such a
solution of the difficulties, except that the recol-

lections of his youth in Rome were such as to have
left an impression compromising not only for his
dignity, but for the solemnity of the coronation. It
is more than probable that besides these disedifying
impressions, he had left at Rome associations and
promises which he was not disposed either to break
or to disavow, such as were recalled to his memory
in later days by Orsini's bombs.

The negociations continued to hang on, but nothing
was decided. The Crimean War broke out; the
Emperor publicly placed his fleet under the protection of our Lady, largely increased the number
of military chaplains, which was recruited in great
measure from the Society of Jesus; in short, his
whole attitude was one to encourage the hopes of
Catholics, and it is certain that in the October of
1854 negociations were again opened between the
Vatican and the Tuileries; their failure, it is equally
certain, was solely due to the maintenance of the
Organic Articles by the Emperor, contrary to his
own sense of right. How different might both his
own history and that of France have been in the
coming years if he had had the true courage of
his convictions! To quote the Marquis de Ségur:
"If Napoleon the Third had had the firmness to
insist on the abolition of the Organic Articles, the
measure would have been hailed with joy by the
mass of the people; he would have been crowned
by the Pope, and the disaster of Sedan, with the
disgrace that followed, might have been spared to

France. At all events, he would have left behind
him a lasting mark of his goodwill to the Church;
his name, in spite of his faults, would have been
dear to Catholics, who would have had him to thank
for their deliverance from that odious legal falsehood
known as the Organic Articles; and, just as the
memory of the first Napoleon is, in spite of Savona
and Fontainebleau, irrevocably linked with that of
the Concordat, so would the memory of Napoleon
the Third, in spite of Castelfidardo, have been
honourably associated with that of the abolition of
the Articles."

And now we must give a very brief account of
the part borne by Mgr. de Sègur in a great work
which he had long had at heart and which he was
happy enough to bring to a successful conclusion—
the restoration of the use of the Roman Liturgy in
the Community and Seminary of Saint-Sulpice.

Slowly and surely the so-called "Gallican liberties" had been languishing and dying out.
Dom Guéranger's pen had done good work in the
right direction; the minds of Catholics tended more
and more strongly towards perfect unity—a tendency
which was to lead up to the definition of the Papal
Infallibility in 1870; in short Gallicanism in *doctrine*
had received its death-blow, What remained to be
dignified with the high-sounding title of "Gallican
liberties" was nothing but a collection of customs
and practices resting on no solid foundation of any
sort, and always disapproved of and regretted by

the Holy See; and among these one of the most
inveterate and least excusable was the abandonment
of the Roman Liturgy. As is well known, the dis-
use of the Roman Breviary was succeeded by the
introduction of diocesan breviaries, all differing from
each other, which was a still more troublesome development of the original evil. Nevertheless, after
the re-establishment of national worship by the
Concordat, these breviaries had become so established
by custom that the Holy See, acting in its usual
spirit of divinely-guided prudence, waited for the
action of time and the grace of God to bring things
straight. The leaven was already at work; and
when Mgr. de Ségur went to Rome in 1852, the
principle of the restoration of the Roman Liturgy
was accepted by the majority of French Catholics.
But the acceptance of a principle is a different thing
from putting it in practice, and the question was
complicated by many difficulties which threatened
to adjourn its solution indefinitely.

As a matter of fact, the great work was not
accomplished in the diocese of Paris till after the
war of 1870; but it was through the instrumentality
of Gaston de Ségur—" Roman," as his brother says,
" from head to foot "—that the reform was adopted
in the Seminary which had trained him for the
priesthood, and to which his attachment was so
great as to earn for him from Pius the Ninth the
playful title of " Monsignor Sulpiziano." His
longings after liturgical unity were shared by many

of the Directors of Saint-Sulpice, notably so by the
great Hebrew scholar, M. le Hir, who hoped great
things from his old pupil's Roman mission. At his
farewell visit he promised to beg from the Holy
Father some favours which the Community greatly
desired, among which was his approbation of several
special offices in use among them. In performing
his promise, Mgr. de Ségur spoke to the Pope of
the decisive influence which the introduction of the
Roman Liturgy in a Seminary receiving pupils
from every diocese could not fail to produce on the
French clergy, and heard from him that he should
greatly rejoice in the example of a return to canonical unity being given by the sons of M. Olier. The
Pope went on to express the pain he felt, not at
any doctrines held at Saint-Sulpice—there was
nothing to blame in this respect—but at the choice
of one or two authors disapproved of at Rome.
Mgr. de Ségur lost no time in informing M. Le Hir
of the Pope's sentiments, and received a reply
from him so touching in its filial sorrow for the
grief caused to their Father by anything done by
the "poor little Community of Saint-Sulpice," so
full of holy humility and entire submission and
obedience to the Holy See, that we wish we had
space to translate it here. Such lessons from such
men deserve pondering in days when many Catholics
are not afraid to discuss and criticise the utterances
of the Vicar of Christ as if they were the expressions
of a private individual. The grief expressed by

Pius the Ninth must have given place to joy on seeing how eagerly his commands were expected, how promptly they would be obeyed ; and he immediately ordered Mgr. de Ségur to write to the Superior, M. Carrière, a clear and formal statemeut of his wishes. The whole correspondence on this subject is so beautiful and so much to the honour of all concerned in it, that it is matter of rejoicing that the Marquis has published it in full in an appendix. We can only give M. Carrière's letter to the Pope, which he sent open to Mgr. de Ségur to hand to him, saying, with characteristic simplicity, " You know so much better than I do the right way of presenting it. I really believe I am the first Superior of Saint-Sulpice who has ever written directly to the Pope."

Most Holy Father,—Prostrate at the feet of Your Holiness the little ecclesiastical Community of Saint-Sulpice receives with the deepest reverence and the most entire submission the expression of your wishes which you have condescended to transmit to us through Mgr. de Ségur. We receive them as commands spoken by the lips of our Lord Jesus Christ, Whom we honour in your sacred person, and we shall conform to them in every particular.

Your Holiness has been already informed that immediately on the appearance of the decrees relative to two writers, one on canon law, the other on theology, whose works were in use in several of our Seminaries, they were at once withdrawn. Now, wherever it depended on us, and especially in Paris, we have sub-stituted for Bailly's theology that of Mgr. Bouvier, corrected according to Your Holiness' intentions. The course of canon law is now oral. I am resolved to be more and more careful that no author whose doctrines are not approved by the Holy See shall be used as a text-book.

As to the Roman Liturgy, our Seminaries have been the first to use it in all the dioceses in which it is adopted. With regard to Paris, your words, Holy Father, have removed all difficulties. The Roman Breviary is to be introduced into our noviceship, and into the Paris Seminary for those subjects not be-longing to the diocese,[1] till the time comes when it may be used by all.

After this assurance of our submission, it is my duty and consolation, Most Holy Father, to express to Your Holiness, in my own name and that of all my brethren, our deep and humble gratitude for the kind permission you have given us to continue to recite the Office proper to the Seminary, as also for the In-dulgence attached to a prayer very dear to us,[2] and for all the other proofs of affection with which you have honoured us. Such proofs must necessarily enkindle more and more in all the members of our community the sentiments of veneration and devotion with which they have always been filled for the Holy Apostolic See and for the august Pontiff who so worthily occupies it, sentiments with which the disciples of M. Olier will

[1] They formed the immense majority at the Seminary of Saint-Sulpice.
[2] The prayer, "O Jesu, vivens in Maria."

always endeavour to inspire all the students in their Seminaries.

Humbly prostrate at the feet of your Holiness, I esteem this a precious opportunity of having the happiness of renewing, in the name of our whole community, the expression of the unalterable reverence, the entire obedience and the absolute devotion with which I am and shall always continue,

Your Holiness' most humble and obedient servant and son in Jesus Christ,

CARRIERE,

Superior of Saint-Sulpice.

Paris, Seminary of Saint-Sulpice,
November 14, 1853.

It is a curious coincidence that, by a kind of instinct, the Emperor was sensible of the logical necessity of that perfect unity in matters of religion which Mgr. de Ségur so largely contributed to bring about in the important work of which we have given a hasty sketch, although the subject in regard to which he manifested his sentiments was a different one. In a letter to Mgr. de Ségur just about the time when the affair of Saint-Sulpice was settled, the Emperor says: "If it were possible to obtain from the Pope the authorization of only one Catechism for the whole of France, I should esteem it a great boon. I should like you to ascertain the mind of His Holiness in this matter."

Curiously enough, the thirty-ninth of the notorious Organic Articles runs thus: "There shall be only one Liturgy and one Catechism for all Catholic churches in France," and it is, perhaps, Mgr. de Ségur remarks, "the only one which has been put into practice by the Holy See in the re-establishment, with the concurrence of the bishops, of the Roman Liturgy: the only one, also, which has been opposed by the different Governments which have succeeded each other in France in the last eighty years, and which they would, one and all, have gladly suppressed."

A year had passed since Gaston de Ségur came to Rome. It had been a time of many blessings. His political functions, with the publicity and the personal consideration and dignity which they involved, were, indeed, a continual trial to him, but the fatherly affection of Pius the Ninth was a powerful makeweight, and his official occupations allowed ample leisure for the apostolic labours of which we have given an imperfect sketch. He had received, as a special grace from God, the happiness of a winter spent with his mother, during which he had revelled in the delight of showing the city to her and others of his family, and now, a few days after their return to France, on the first day of our Lady's own month, she reminded him of his covenant with her on the occasion of his first Mass. We will give the account in the words of his friend, Mgr. de Conny, who arrived at Rome just as Madame de Ségur left it.

I arrived on the 25th of April, and on that day my friend told me that there always seemed to be a red

G

spot before one of his eyes, at the outer corner. I
said it was no doubt the effect of the beginning of the
warm weather, but he continued to complain of the
sensation, and on the 1st of May, after a meeting of
the Rota, as he sat down to his painting for a recrea-
tion, suddenly the red spot spread like a curtain before
the whole field of vision. 'There is one eye gone,' he
said, 'and very soon I shall lose the other.' I made
him come with me at once to Dr. Mayer, the physician
of the French Army of Occupation, who did not
conceal the gravity of the matter. . . . then we went
to walk in the streets bordering the Quirinal Gardens.
I was overwhelmed by this blow, while he was perfectly calm. 'God,' he said, 'gave me two eyes thirty-
three years ago ; to-day He has taken back one of them,
and soon, I expect, He will take the other. I have
only to thank Him for the time He has allowed
them to me. He is the Master.' 'Of course,' I answered, 'those are the sentiments of faith, but one cannot be insensible to the impressions of nature.' 'Are
we Christians, are we priests,' he exclaimed, 'that
we should yield to the impressions of nature when
faith speaks?' I could not help thinking that if any
one had been near enough to hear our conversation,
he would have thought that it was I who had just
received a great blow, and that my friend was consoling me under it, but doing so in rather an austere
manner. He went on : 'All this is very good for me :
in my position, treated, as I am, so kindly by the
Pope and with so much confidence by the Emperor,
I could hardly have escaped being shortly made Arch-

bishop and Cardinal; and do what one may, even ecclesiastical dignities do expose a man to the danger of being uplifted in his heart. Now I shall be clear of all that, and go back to Paris to hear the confessions of my poor fellows there, which will be much better for me.' His only sorrow in the matter was the thought of his mother's grief; yet for her, too, He Who brings ' all good things from evil ' made her son's blindness a fruitful source of blessings. As he says in the little book which he dedicated to her memory after her death: ' This blessed infirmity, so severe apparently, so good and sanctifying in reality, was the occasion of my return to Paris, and to my mother whom I never left, except occasionally, during the eighteen years which God had in store for her: and the same cause gained for me from the affection of Pius the Ninth a priceless boon which my mother shared with me to the end of her life—I mean the permission of having the Blessed Sacrament in my chapel.'

This permission was, indeed, a favour very rarely granted, and, it may be added, rarely solicited, and when Mgr. de Ségur made the request, the Pope hesitated for an instant; then, conquered by the expression of sadness on the suppliant's face, he bent over him as he knelt, and taking his head between his hands, said, in a voice of intense affection: " I should refuse most people, but I say ' yes ' to you because of my love for you " *(perchè vi voglio bene)*, then he added, in Latin, *Ad consolationem, ad*

tempus: thinking, as he then did, that there were
hopes of a cure; but this was not to be, and the
time for which this supreme consolation was to last
was to be the lifetime of the saintly sufferer.
Several persons, both in Rome and elsewhere, were
very urgent with him to implore a miraculous cure
from God, but he never would consent. He could
not even bring himself to desire anything but what
God sent, and he always expressed the strongest
conviction of the spiritual benefits he should derive
from this visitation of God. " It is a serious thing
and a great responsibility," he once said, " to be the
subject of a miracle, and I should be afraid of it."

Never once, either in conversation or in his letters,
did Gaston de Ségur express the slightest distress or
self-pity under the trial he was enduring, a trial,
moreover, which he knew to be the forerunner of a
greater one, for he never doubted that he was about
to be completely blind. The ecclesiastical dignities
which he foresaw he must soon relinquish were,
indeed, a burden which he was thankful to lay down,
but there was not even a passing sigh for the art
which had been the passion of his youth and which
was still his one relaxation. No one ever surprised
a look of sadness on his face, or detected the slightest
change in the cheerful serenity which was his
distinguishing characteristic. There was always the
same even tranquillity, the same sweet courtesy and
unselfish consideration for others, the same forgetfulness of self; and so, insensibly, all who knew him

began to feel confident that the mischief was only temporary. The Emperor was so persuaded of this, that he discussed with the Bishop of Amiens and others the question whether it would be possible to make Mgr. de Ségur Grand Almoner of France, a dignity which he had serious thoughts of restoring, if, indeed, that state of mind can be called serious which was always characterized by a certain sloth-fulness, or rather *nonchalance*, which joined to his real ignorance on such matters, made him abandon many far more important projects and reforms, to which he was personally inclined, in compliance with the wretched policy of his nearest advisers. The prospect, however vague, of being destined to such a post would have been alarming to Mgr. de Ségur if he had ever shared the illusions of those around him as to the future. But he remembered his agreement with our Lady, and he knew that this was her answer. Once when a friend inquired about his sight, he answered playfully, " My eye no longer belongs to me ; our Lady has taken it and sent it to Purgatory in my stead." He had taken the first step on the *Via Dolorosa* which the mercy of God, so he called it in his noble and childlike spirit of faith, had appointed for him, and he never doubted that he should walk in it to the end. Fifteen months were to pass before his blindness became complete, and he spent them in a calm and cheerful preparation for the night of which this twi-light was the herald. He began, by degrees and

without a word to any one, to practise walking
and helping himself in different ways while keeping
his eyes closed, and he succeeded so well, that when
the time of blindness came, it was found that he
was able to shave himself as adroitly as when he
was in the full possession of his eyesight. Day
by day he accustomed himself to use his sight less
in saying Mass, and as he had the Pope's permission
always to say a Votive Mass of our Lady, he learned
it by heart, as well as an immense number of psalms,
offices, and other devotions which he had habitually
recited. His memory had, up to this time, been
anything but good, so that it was a difficulty to him
to quote accurately a verse of the Sacred Scriptures
or a passage from the Fathers ; and surely it must
have been by a special help from the Master he
trusted so absolutely that, from the time we are
speaking of to the end of his life, he was in the
habit of making long quotations in his sermons and
instructions with a fidelity and readiness which were
remarkable. He also learned by heart all the Masses
de tempore of the Blessed Virgin, as well as those of
the Holy Ghost, the Blessed Sacrament, the Sacred
Heart, the Cross, the Chair of St. Peter, the Stig-
mata of St. Francis, the Patronage of St. Francis
of Sales, and the Mass for the Dead. To the
end of his life, too, he gave Communion at his
Mass, and no accident ever occurred to distress
either himself or his communicants. " Give and it
shall be given to you." Gaston de Ségur had

given himself unreservedly to God, and these were
"added" graces by which the Heavenly King
"delighted to honour" the faithful servant who
sought, first and solely, his Master's justice and the
interests of His Kingdom. And so the weeks and
months went on, and while the many who loved and
venerated him were hoping for his cure and dreaming
of new duties and dignities in the future, he was
waiting calmly and prayerfully for the next touch of
God's hand which was to close his eyes for ever in
this world to the light of day.

The month of July, 1854, found Mgr. de Ségur at
Les Nouettes, where he was passing the vacation
with his mother. He felt so sure that the crisis was
at hand, that he made it a special request to our
Lady, to be allowed to see his brothers and sisters
once more before the curtain fell between him and
all outward things. His prayer was heard : there
was absolutely no reason why all the members of
his large and scattered family should assemble at
their father's house at that particular time—yet so
it was. His brother and biographer arrived the last
of all, on the 1st of September, and on the 2nd, a
Saturday, the blow fell. A doctor in the neighbourhood, a friend of the family, who had examined
Gaston's eyes the day before, called early in the
morning to dissect before him the eye of an ox,
which the physician had described to him as re-
markably beautiful in its structure. He was greatly
interested, and after breakfast the whole family went

out to walk in the grounds. He was rather in advance of the rest, with one of his brothers; quite suddenly he stood still, saying, " I am blind," adding immediately a particular request that nothing should be said to his mother till it was unavoidable. She came into his room more than once in the course of the day, and he talked to her so naturally and cheer- fully, that she had no suspicion of the truth; it was not till dinner-time, when she noticed that one of his sisters cut up his food, that it broke upon her. One can well believe that, as the Marquis says, none of those present ever forgot the scene, the bitter grief of all but the sufferer, the contrast between natural human anguish and Divine supernatural serenity. The following extract from a letter written four days later to Mgr. Pie, gives so beautiful a picture of his state of mind, that we cannot resist quoting it.

Happily, I am just now with my poor mother, my brothers and sisters, whose grief is a greater trouble to me than my small individual trials. The cross is such a good and holy thing that only a very poor sort of Christian would dare to complain of it, and if no one but myself were concerned, I should be more apt to rejoice than lament. In life and in death are we not altogether our Lord's? And what does it matter, after all, whether we see the light of this world or not, if only the eyes of our soul are enlightened so as to see the True Eternal Light, Jesus Christ, dwelling in us? Remember me, my dear lord, at the holy altar, at the feet of that Divine Master, and pray that I may carry His holy Cross as I ought. As you may suppose, all the fine plans which had been made for or against me are come to nothing. My vocation is simplified, and the will of God, the only rule to be followed in all this, is made plain. I only pray that the Emperor may make a good choice when the time comes and that he may have near him a man devoted to Holy Church and to France. For my part, I shall return to Rome, where my life will not be much changed by my new infirmity, I can carry on my uninteresting labours of the Rota by my hearing only, and I have a little priestly ministry in working order. One only needs one's tongue, ears, and legs, to preach and hear confessions. Perhaps it will be quite a stroke of luck for big sinners of the bashful sort to be able to tell their story to a confessor who cannot see anything. But for this accident of mine, I should have made it my duty and pleasure to ask your hospitality for a few days at Poitiers; as it is, I am difficult to move, and must not run about any more. Farewell for the present, my dear and kind Bishop, I embrace you with all my heart, and can love you very much, thank God, without seeing you.

It must not be thought, however, that Mgr. de Ségur had no natural shrinking from suffering, no opportunity for practising the virtue of resignation: the cross weighed heavily, gladly as he bore it, and this mingling of sorrow and joy is evident in many of his letters. " This is a grand day with me," he writes on the 2nd of September, to a young Fran-

ciscan novice; " it is thirteen years since I became
quite blind, since our good and merciful God forced
me to enter a little portable cloister, of which only
He can break the enclosure." To his sister Sabine
he writes : " The Gospel says, ' If thy eye be single,
thy whole body shall be lightsome.' Now, my eye
is more than that. I have there my little monastery,
my moveable cloister, which binds me to poverty
and obedience ; to poverty, by cutting me off from
everything whether I will or no; to obedience, by
making me continually dependent on some one
the whole day long. Blessed be God! Ask Him
always to be merciful to me, and to keep me on
the Cross, close beside Him, like the good thief."
And again : " It is a great blessing, a priceless boon,
to be fastened to the Cross by any infirmity, above
all by blindness; it is a continual participation in
the Crucifixion of Jesus, and a kind of religious
consecration which compels you to renounce the
world with all its insane delights. . . . It is like a
drop of heavenly wormwood which *christianizes* every
draught which the world offers, an elixir, as it were,
against naturalism." What he loved, in his blindness, then, was the Will of God, the Cross of Christ,
the means of giving himself more exclusively to the
salvation of souls ; but none the less, his joyous
cheerfulness through that night of twenty-seven
years was one long act of heroic virtue.

To Gaston's family, and his many devoted friends
resignation was more difficult. His poor father

cannot believe that God will send so terrible a trial as blindness to " his good and holy son, the blessing of the whole family, who has always made so good a use of his eyesight."

Mgr. Bastide writes to Madame de Ségur from Rome that he is ready to believe that God will cure his friend by a miracle, because, if there are few who can bear adversity well, there are fewer still who can stand the test of honours and dignities, and that Mgr. de Ségur, being one of that rare sort, he cannot but believe him destined to do a great work for God in a high position. And Louis Veuillot, in a letter worthy of that great writer, says that after all he persists " in hoping that there is hope left, and that the oculists, and, after or before the oculists, the saints of God will do something for this sad state of things."

M. Gay, who regards the question altogether from the spiritual point of view, writes : " I bless God for the peace He has given you in circumstances in which so many would be cast down. I quite understand what you say about the leisure your condition gives you for thinking of the only real good. In truth, a Christian is never blind. ' He Who commanded the light to shine out of darkness hath shined in our hearts,' and for one who has that light, the darkness itself is as bright as day."

But the soul which beyond all others rose, strong and steadfast to the heights of courageous sanctity at this time of trial was the saintly Countess

Rostopchine, whose long life of more than eighty years was drawing to a close in almost incessant prayer and communion with God. She had rejoiced with a full heart over her grandson's conversion and vocation, his labours and apostolic work in Rome ; and now, with a still more fervent thankfulness she rejoiced in the " fiery trial " by which the great Lover of souls was perfecting the one so dear to Him. We will give an extract from a letter to her daughter and grandson, written a month after he was struck with complete blindness :

Moscow, October 12.

My dear Sophie, my dear Gaston,—An illness, which has been, however, neither long nor painful, has hindered me from answering you. Gaston is, then, very dear to God, since He has sent him a trial so severe as the loss of sight. I look upon it as a pledge of Divine grace, which only tries him in order to crown his submission, his faith, his love for God, his filial piety. Ah, my daughter ! how happy are you to be the mother of a saint.

My son, my dear and precious son, you have been struck down like St. Paul ; nay, if I dared say so, more blessedly even, since it was not when you were persecuting Jesus Christ, but when you were seeking His glory, and the good of your neighbour. I ought rather to ask your blessing than to give you mine ; and yet I do bless you in my character of an old woman, of a worshipper of the God you worship, of your grandmother, and of one of the poor of our Lord, before Whom, thanks to my age and His mercy, I hope very soon to stand.

As the Marquis de Ségur says, "This is indeed the letter of a saint to a saint, and one seems to be listening to an echo of the voice of Felicitas or Symphorosa, encouraging her children to martyrdom." And in the words of Mgr. de Ségur to his sister, we may ask, "Is not the martyrdom of life sometimes as sharp as that of death?"

Mgr. de Ségur, though at once and absolutely refusing to realize any of the visions of ecclesiastical dignities which so many of his friends cherished for him, or rather for the interests of the Church through him, did not immediately resign his official position at Rome. Great medical authorities persisted in the opinion that the cause of his blindness was a simple cataract curable by an operation, and he himself was almost alone in maintaining a contrary conviction. He thought too, with the Christian prudence so beautifully allied in him with enthusiastic fervour, that his definitive resolution would be more safely and wisely formed after longer delay; accordingly he returned to Rome, where his life, for the next fifteen months, was much the same as before, except for the limitations made necessary by his infirmity.

One immense joy was his shortly after his return to Rome, that of being there for the glorious 8th of

December, 1854. He was present at all the ceremonies which preceded and followed the proclamation of the dogma, and it was with indescrable
emotion that, standing among the hundred thousand
candles in St. Peter's, to whose light his eyes were
shut, he heard the voice of Pius IX. declare that
Mary was Immaculate in her Conception: the
memory of that day was the illumination of the
rest of his life.

A few days after this great day, Mgr. de Ségur
had a heavy sorrow to endure in the death of a
cousin, Louis de Villeneuve, a young naval officer
to whom he was greatly attached, and with whom
he had kept up a regular correspondence ever since
he left France for the Crimea. He died, very
suddenly, under the walls of Eupatoria: his mother's
despair was heart-rending, and, like all his family,
it was to Mgr. de Ségur that she turned for the
consolation he was always so ready and able to
give. On a picture, found in the young officer's
"Following of Christ," he had written on the day
of his First Communion, "Gaston de Ségur came
to Orleans: he has taught me to love God without
slavish fear. His advice was this: purity, filial
love, consolation sought from our Blessed Lady,
daily prayer." Faithful to the end to what the
Marquis calls "this brief and holy programme,"
death found his young cousin, as the chaplain of
his ship bore witness, surprised indeed, but not
unprepared.

It was a great happiness to Mgr. de Ségur during these last months of his Roman residence to find the French army of occupation, officers and soldiers alike, animated by a truly Christian spirit which had come out very brightly in the autumn of this year when the terrible scourge of the cholera made so many victims in the little army. The following characteristic extract from a letter of their brave chaplain's, tells of the Pope's visit to the cholera hospital and how the Abbé Bastide became Mgr. Bastide.

Rome, September 24, 1854.

My very dear friend,

At four o'clock last Friday, when we least expected it, the Holy Father came to visit our poor cholera patients at the hospital Santa Teresa. You have no idea what efforts were made to make the Pope give up an action so useful and edifying to all: thanks to Xavier de Mérode, the Holy Father's goodness of heart and piety won the day. It must be owned that Xavier worked away as he never did before—so I leave you to judge! He must have made the whole Papal Court tremble more than ever this time at his plain-speaking, and the visit was a regular triumph for him ; you could see it in his face, which was as radiant as Pio Nono's. Some of our soldiers were motionless, open-mouthed—dumb with astonishment : others showed their joy very touchingly, crossing themselves devoutly as the Holy Father drew near. One poor *chasseur de Vincennes* who had got right after a very wild life, whose confession I had just heard, instantly held out a common blue glass rosary to be blessed. I think the Pope was taken with his honest face, he came up to him, showed him especial tenderness and said, " Take this medal quickly, my child ; it is the only one I have with me, and I do not want to make the rest jealous." · Speaking of faces, I can give you no idea of the good X......'s : he had come post-haste from Sant' Andrea, to receive the Pope. He was pale and blue at the same time, so that I could not help crying out : " The Pope will give him the cholera ! " " *Ma, davvero,*" said the Holy Father, " it looks like it ! " To be brief, our friend, the doctor, the officer on guard, chaplain, infirmarians, all were evidently touched by the presence of the Holy Father, who spent a good half-hour with us. M. Coytier, as he escorted him out, said very gracefully : " Holy Father, all France, above all her army, will thank you for the noble and courageous action you have just performed." Then the Pope turned round : we were all on our knees at the entrance of the Hospital, and the street Quattro-Fontane was full of people : " May God reward you," he said as he went away, " for what you have done : may He bless you and give you strength always to do your duties well."

Now, Monseigneur, you must know that after this visit, which should have brought us nothing but blessings, your humble servant and friend, in consequence of being among the cholera-patients, has suddenly turned *rather purple*. It is my throat which is affected. Now, do not be alarmed, there is nothing serious in my condition. The truth is just this: yesterday, as we were quietly sitting at supper, Xavier de Mérode sent his new servant, (a kind of bat he has discovered among the ruins of Santa-Balbina) with a huge paper from Mgr. de Medici announcing my appointment as cameriere to His Holiness. I believe these camerieri are the same who walk all in red at the *Corpus Domini* procession. I thought at first that it was Xavier's doing, and I really was rather glad, because it is a certificate from the Pope that I was not afraid of danger, but when I saw Xavier come the next minute to pull a nice new *collerino* from my neck and give me his own instead—a ragged concern, but a purple one !—I was touched, because I was assured that this idea was the Holy Father's own. Indeed, Xavier called his attention to the fact that this dignity was a difficult one to accept and to bear in France—but the Pope said "O never mind, the Abbé Bastide has plenty of sense, he will bear it as it ought to be borne." And those words are a thousand times more to me than any imaginable titles.

The title was, however, far from being an empty honour: all the army knew the history of it ; and his influence and the good it enabled him to do were much increased in consequence. Mgr. de Ségur had a great wish for his friend's *prestige* to be still further enhanced by the Cross of the Legion of Honour. He knew that Napoleon III. had the intention of sending it to himself, and he now wrote

H

to the Emperor positively declining the Cross, and begging him to transfer it to Mgr. Bastide, the Christian-soldier so worthy to wear it. He succeeded in the end, but not for some time: it was not till two years later that his petition was granted.

CHAPTER VI.

Apostolate in Paris.

IT was on the 29th of January, the feast of St. Francis of Sales, 1856, that Mgr. de Ségur, after holding the office of Auditor of the Rota in Rome for four years, took possession of the apartment in the Rue du Bac, in which the remaining twenty-five years of his life were spent. He had felt it his duty to make a fair trial of the condition in which his blindness placed him, to judge calmly as to the best way of serving God under these circumstances, and the result was a firm conviction that his proper sphere was Paris, among the soldiers, workmen, and little ones to whom the first-fruits of his priesthood had been dedicated.

No sooner was his course clear than his resignation was a settled thing; but before it could be accepted by the Pope and the Emperor it was necessary to arrange his future position in a manner suitable to the high functions he had discharged, his standing in Rome, and the requirements of his infirmity. A canonry of the first order of the Chapter of Saint Denys seemed all that could be desired, but there were difficulties. All the canons of the first order are bishops, and it is contrary to canon law for a blind man to receive episcopal consecration. This difficulty was met by a Papal brief conferring on Mgr. de Ségur the office of Apostolic Protonotary, with all the dignities and privileges which are enjoyed by members of the episcopal order ; thus enabling the French Government to appoint him to the canonry. The life of the Roman prelate was closed, the Catholic mission of Mgr. de Ségur in France was to begin, In the twenty-five years that followed, the only changes were the consequence of the growth cf his apostolate, with the exception of occasional visits to Rome ; and henceforward his biographer ceases to follow any chronological order, presenting us, instead, with a series of pictures from the life which was now filled to overflowing with incessant and multiplied labours in the Master's vineyard,

The Abbé Louis Klingenhoffen accompanied him as his secretary, in which capacity he remained till his return to Rome on his admission to the priest-hood, He was succeeded by the Abbé Diringer, whose name is inseparable from that of the venerable prelate, to whom he was eyes and hand for more than twenty years. The following extract is from a letter in which Mgr. de Ségur describes his view of their relations :

My dear Abbé,—Just another month of vacation, and you will be my slave, I shall do my best, for, and in the love of our Lord, to lighten the task, which will at times be both difficult and wearisome in consequence of the infirmity which God in His mercy, has sent me, and you, on your side, will try from the same motive, to bear my daily imperfections, and to carry that part of the cross which will rest on your shoulders. . . . We shall live as priests should—that is to say, simply, laboriously, and rather hardly. May God bless you, and increase in both of us His Divine charity.

Hardly less important than the choice of a secretary was that of a personal attendant, and here too Mgr. de Ségur was singularly fortunate. He had been greatly struck in Rome by a young soldier, whose upright manly character and childlike piety influenced many of his comrades in a remarkable way. Méthol, that was his name, was encouraged to come to the Palazzo Brancadoro, and the more this simple loyal soul became known to his host, the more he valued and trusted him, so that when his return to Paris was determined, Mgr. de Ségur proposed to take him into his service. Méthol was the eldest of a Basque family, and in that part of France, in defiance of the civil code, the old traditions were kept up by which the paternal inheritance fell to the eldest son, whose duty it was to provide for the rest. In order to attach himself to Mgr. de Ségur, therefore, it was necessary for Méthol to resign his right of primogeniture to his next brother. This he did without hesitation, the happiness of

living with the priest he had loved and venerated in
Rome made up for any sacrifice.   Méthol entered
the house in the Rue du Bac at the same time as
his master : and to the day of his death was the
very model of a faithful servant.   That long and
loving service included many varied offices : he was
treasurer, man of business, confidant and administrator of his master's charities.   It was a difficult
post in many ways, requiring at least as much tact
and intelligence as goodwill ; but the Marquis bears
testimony to the perfect manner in which its duties
were discharged ; and in comparing Méthol with the
faithful servant of the Saint to whom Mgr. de Ségur
was so devoted, and to whom he bore so great a
resemblance, speaks of him as having been "another
Rolland to another Francis of Sales."   It is worth
while, in days when the Christian relations between
master and servant are so little understood, to give
an extract from a letter in which Mgr. de Ségur
gives his views on the subject :

I add a few words to my brother's letter, my dear
good Méthol, in order to make things quite clear, and
to tell you what I expect of you if you take service
with me.   What I desire *above all* in the two men I
mean to employ, of whom you shall, if you like, be one,
is a regular Christian life, more like that of religious
than of ordinary servants, and also the assurance that
they are happy with me, and that they will remain
with me all my life.   I want them to see in me not a
master who pays them, but a father they obey from

respect and affection for the love of God. Of course this does not imply that I shall not pay you regular wages, which my brother's last letter has clearly explained: but, once more, these wages and everything connected with them are only to be secondary considerations with both of us. It is a brother and a son I want to have about me. I know this is not the way in which masters and servants usually look at things; and that is why I urge it upon you, my dear Méthol, to reflect soberly before making up your mind, so that there may be no disappointment afterwards. You see, it is an important step to decide upon: let me hear directly you have done so. . . . Now, my friend, adieu, and whatever your resolution may be, you may be sure that I shall always feel as kindly towards you as now.

The other servant whom Mgr. de Ségur engaged was an old comrade of Méthol's, a Basque like himself; he too remained in his service to the end of his life.

A few words, now, of the apartment in the Rue du Bac, which Christian piety still reveres as a sanctuary. It is the second floor; the stairs are worn by the feet of the countless visitors who came and went for five-and-twenty years. The first object that meets the eye on entering is a large statue of our Lady, before which a lamp is always burning. Mgr. de Ségur never returned home without saying a 'Hail Mary' on his knees before the image of her whom he spoke of as "the

Mistress of the house." The sitting-room looks over a small garden to the church of St. Thomas d'Aquin, and the blind prelate delighted in being able to assist at the offices of his parish church without leaving home. His real "home" was the chapel; and the number of hours which he passed there, day and night, in adoration before the Blessed Sacrament, is known only to God and His angels. There is something very beautiful and touching in his care and anxiety to adorn and beautify for the Master dwelling there the chapel which his own eyes never saw. "Let us do our very best;" he writes during one of his absences from Paris to the faithful Méthol, who was charged with the superintendence of some improvements; "if we lodge our Lord as well as ever we can here, there will be a chance of His doing the same for us in Paradise."

Mgr. de Ségur rose for some years at six, but as he grew older and slept less, the time was changed to five. While dressing, he was in the habit of reciting prayers and psalms—"there really seemed no end to them," the good Méthol used to say. Then he went to the chapel, where, on Saturdays and Sundays, some penitents would have been waiting since six o'clock. His meditation was made before rising, in order not to delay the confessions which always occupied him up to the moment of Mass, and were resumed directly after it. More than once, on the eves of great feasts, he had to deprive himself of saying Mass, his penitents succeeding each other without intermission from six till eleven o'clock. Ordinarily, he did not hear confessions after nine, unless Méthol, as sometimes happened, was persuaded to plead for some privileged persons, that is to say, some "big sinners."

After hearing confessions, Mgr. de Ségur was occupied with his secretary till midday, when he breakfasted; then came visits of charity in the interest of his many good works, on returning from which they both made a visit to the Blessed Sacrament, and said Vespers together before leaving the chapel. Then, writing again, unless it was an afternoon for confessions. Saturdays were entirely given up to his penitents. He heard confessions at the Collége Stanislas from eleven to three, and in his own chapel the rest of the day, the young clerks and apprentices keeping him in the confessional often till nearly eleven at night. Except on Saturdays, Mgr. de Ségur dined with his parents at half-past six, and remained with them till nine, when he said night prayers with his secretary and servants in the chapel. After his mother's death, he worked till seven, and seldom went out anywhere to dinner, the time which had till then been given to his family being restored to God. Such was the usual daily routine, but in the first years of his residence in Paris, while he was in health and full vigour, there were many exceptions to the rule.

From one end of the city to the other there were innumerable claims upon him, and he was summoned, now to a Patronage festivity, now to a workman's *soirée*, or Catholic *cercle*, or a distribution of prizes; there were sermons, retreats, and missions, too; often in far-distant *faubourgs*. On such occasions he made a point of doing honour to his guests, by wearing his purple cassock and the order of his chapter, and poor Madame de Ségur's heart sank when he came to dine with her thus attired. She knew it meant the loss of his company for the evening for her, and a good deal of extra fatigue for him, but she loved God and His poor too well not to make her sacrifice very willingly.

To conclude this imperfect sketch of a life altogether filled by God, we may add that Gaston de Ségur never went out, however often or however hastily he might be called upon to do so, without entering his chapel to kiss the ground and make one rapid fervent act of adoration to the Divine Master of his house and his soul.

The first good work which occupied Mgr. de Ségur on his return to Paris was the one which always held the first place in his affections, the Patronages of apprentices; the very day after his arrival he opened a retreat at the house of our Lady of Nazareth, but it was the Patronage of the Rue de Grenelle to which, as it was close at hand, he devoted himself most completely. The council of this house was composed of the best and most pious of the lads themselves, under the wise and prudent guidance of the excellent Frère Baudime. One of the priests of St. Thomas d'Aquin was their voluntary chaplain, and the Patronage had gradually become the centre of Christian life for the youths engaged in business or workshops throughout the Faubourg St. Germain. The work, already thoroughly organized and flourishing, received a fresh impulse, and acquired a more extensive development from Mgr. de Ségur's personal influence and the irresistible charm by which he always won the hearts of the young. He was the life of the weekly and quarterly meetings, and all were welcomed to the house in the Rue du Bac as freely and affectionately as were the noisy visitors in the Rue Cassette in the early days of Gaston de Ségur's priesthood. Every Sunday he said Mass for them and gave them an instruction, receiving all who had anything to say to him privately afterwards. His name was a household word among them, and so, unconsciously, they too became his coadjutors in the apostolic work. Their companions were eager to see and know this wonderful blind prelate who was so holy and kind and cheery, so ready to comfort and to forgive, who knew always how to say the right thing whether one was merry or sad : and so, they too fell under the charm, and the circle spread and widened. The quarterly meetings were something special : only the members and their families were admitted, and Mgr. de Ségur never failed to provide the attraction of good music or little dramatic scenes and recitations. With his own simple grace and courtesy he called on several of the most distinguished *artistes* of Paris, to ask this favour of them "for the love of God and the poor," as though the subject were as familiar to them as to himself; and his request never failed to meet with a ready and generous consent.

Besides the abundant help these concerts and recitations brought to his different *œuvres,* Mgr. de Ségur liked to get acquainted with the artist world ; most of those who composed it were, indeed, absolutely without religion, but nearly all were liberal and kind-hearted, and he knew that there was no surer way of benefiting their souls than by leading them to help the poor. Like Sœur Rosalie, he delighted in this interchange of material and spiritual alms, and he used to say that by moving these generous hearts to works of charity he might very likely be preparing the way for Christian deaths. Among the great *artistes* who were most ready to give their help, honourable mention is made of Roger, Faure, and Mme. Carvalho. After a very brilliant and successful concert, at which they had sung, Mgr. de Ségur called on them to express his gratitude and gave them all a handsomely bound copy of the "*Réponses.*" One of the party, a Jew, was naturally omitted, but he appealed to Mgr. de Ségur against his exclusion, and begged for the *souvenir,* which, of course, he

received.   Mme. Carvalho's copy became historical :
when acting for the first time the part of Marguerite
in " Faust," which she made so peculiarly her own,
she objected to use a missal for the Church scene,
and took up the copy of the " *Réponses* " instead.
Perhaps she thought it had brought her luck :
anyhow, she would never use another book for
this scene, which was her companion at 300
representations.

Before long, Mgr. de Ségur had established,
among the most pious of the members, a little conference of St. Vincent of Paul.   He never missed
one of the meetings, and trained the young Brothers
himself in the science of corporal and spiritual
almsgiving.   It was a work after his own heart,
this fostering of "the charities of poor to poor,"
and never was he happier than when talking to
these dear children of his about their work, thus,
as the Marquis beautifully says, "making charity
the safeguard of their faith and perseverance."
And he did not forget the rich children, either : he
formed a sort of association among them by which
they became the patrons of his apprentices and
poor.   They had their meetings in the house in
the Rue du Bac, each child contributing an alms
of a hundred francs yearly, part of which they had
to raise by a *quête* among their friends.   In this way
nearly two thousand francs were collected yearly.

The fatherly affection of Mgr. de Ségur accompanied his "patronage children" throughout their

lives.   He exerted himself to find suitable places
for them, he officiated at their marriages, baptized
their children, visited and consoled them in sickness
and prepared them for the last sacraments.   Often
and often after a death in a poor family, he would
return later in the evening to take his turn of
watching and praying beside the dead, and unless
it was absolutely impossible, he always joined the
humble train of mourners at the funeral.

, There are many who remember the death of a
young workman, one of the dearest of Mgr. de
Ségur's children, who had been, from childhood,
the model of a young Christian ; the blind prelate
followed the coffin, giving his arm to the poor father,
all the members of the Patronage walking behind.
A murmur of affection and admiration ran through
the crowd of spectators at the sight of the tall figure,
bare-headed, supporting and at the same time guided
by the father of young Athanase Rousselle, and
when the humble procession set out from Saint-
Sulpice to the cemetery, it made its way through
a densely packed crowd.   No wonder that, twenty-
four years later, the inhabitants of ·the *quartier*
thronged to Notre Dame to return to the apostle
of the poor working men of Paris the same respectful offices which he had so often paid to them.
One little detail—the more touching for its littleness
—which the Marquis gives in speaking of Athanase
is this : Mgr. de Ségur knew that it was his custom
to bring his mother an almond-cake every year on

her feast, and from the death of her boy till her own, poor Madeleine Rousselle received one every 22nd of July, in the name of her dead son, from him who had been so true a father to him.

There were, of course, many who, in the dangèrs and temptations of Paris, forgot the pious lessons of their boyhood and wandered far away from the safe shelter of the fold. But, sooner or later, the strayed sheep came back. He used to say it was *always* so; the impression made by his words and example, and by his unwearied devotion, was never effaced. Sometimes it would be a time of trial, sometimes the purifying effect of an honest affection, sometimes the pressure of sickness or the shadow of death, by which God's grace spoke to their hearts: and then, whether they arose, like the prodigal, and went to their father, or whether he sought them out, they were sure of the same glad welcome: he never despaired of any one, he never doubted that he should win back to Christ the souls that had once known the sweetness of His yoke: what wonder then, that such victories were gained by the unfailing charity that "hopeth all things?" Side by side with his work among the Patronages was one for the young of a different class; we allude to his devoted labours among the pupils of the Collège Stanislas, labours which occupied him nearly to the end of his life, but on which it is scarcely necessary to dwell in this brief sketch, as, making the requisite allowance for the difference of

class, they were much the same as those in the
Patronage. But a few words must be said of a
work very dear to the heart of Mgr. de Ségur, that
of discovering and developing ecclesiastical vocations. This is, comparatively at least, easy when
the recruits for the priesthood are of the upper
class, but in the case of a working lad it is a case
beset with difficulties. There is the danger of
the dawning vocation being extinguished in the
poisonous atmosphere of a Paris workshop, there is
the opposition of parents, who dread the prospect
of years of sacrifice which must be faced, and the
loss of the wages when the young apprentice should
have become a journeyman. What Mgr. de Ségur
did in this way is incalculable, he never suffered a
vocation to languish for lack of development, no
matter what obstacles were in the way. He charged
himself with bringing the education of the boys up
to the point necessary for admission to the " Little
Seminary," and his ingenuity in finding tutors
willing to teach the rudiments of Latin gratis was
something wonderful. He provided the necessary
pension, consecrating to this object most of the
income proceeding from his writings—amounting
sometimes to more than ten thousand francs a year
—he induced rich and pious families to adopt several
of his *protégés* by engaging to pay for one or more,
formed associations of ladies to collect subscriptions
for the same purpose, and gladly became himself a
beggar, to feed, clothe and train the future priests

of the sanctuary. In several dioceses the affection of the bishops facilitated the matter greatly: this was especially the case in that of Poitiers, thanks to the warm attachment of the illustrious Mgr. Pie; and the Seminary of Montmorillon was the one he loved best, and which received the largest number of his spiritual children.

He had a great gift of discernment in this matter: if he did not discover very marked signs of a vocation in any of the youths at the Collége Stanislas who consulted him on the subject, he quietly told the boy not to enter on the question till his school-days were over. "It is never well to precipitate these matters of vocation, it is like gathering unripe fruit," he wrote to one of these good lads, who was anxious to settle the matter off hand, and who afterwards became an excellent husband and father. "I advise you to dismiss this important affair till your studies are completed, till you are a man and have to choose your state of life: till then your vocation is to be a good student, pure, honourable and God-fearing; just keep to that." To another he wrote: "Do not think about your vocation: it is so much lost time: when you have to decide God will enlighten you. Till then, remain quiet and go on living from day to day with a good conscience and good will."

But when he knew, by Divine illumination, that the Master's call was clear and certain, he was not afraid to *brusquer* things with a courage and confi-

I

dence always justified by the event. Once, a youth
of seventeen consulted him on this subject. His
previous director had put him off for a long time
from one confession to another, not considering it
a pressing matter. Mgr. de Ségur questioned him
closely, prayed earnestly, and at their second interview said: "Well now, my dear boy, we have got
to Easter; you must finish the year of study, and
enter the Seminary of Issy after the vacation." The
lad, though startled by a promptitude and decision
for which he was hardly prepared, accepted the
answer as the order of Providence and obeyed to
the letter. He never ceased to bless God for leading him to "the blind saint," and he is now one
of the most admirable priests in France.

One day, Mgr. de Ségur received a visit from the
Abbé Millot, Superior of the Ecclesiastical College
of Saint-Dizier, who came to offer him the sum of
sixty thousand francs if he was willing to undertake
the re-establishment of the little community of
"Clerics of St. Sulpice," which, after many vicissi-
tudes, had been dispersed after the revolution of
1830. The matter was the more pressing from the
fact that the two Little Seminaries of Paris were
compelled by different circumstances to receive
boys whose vocations had not been sufficiently
tested. The offer was unhesitatingly accepted, on
the condition that M. Millot obtained the formal
and entire approval of Cardinal Morlot, the Archbishop of Paris. This was willingly given, a house

was taken at Auteuil, and M. Millot began the work by receiving gratuitously, in honour of the twelve Apostles, twelve boys whose singular piety left little doubt of their perseverance. Mgr. de Ségur joined heart and soul in this good work, and became the very life of the little community both at Auteuil and at Issy, whither it was shortly moved.

Already one is induced to ask how it was possible for one man, and that man blind, to carry on all these ceaseless and absorbing works: and yet this was not all, for before he had spent quite two years in the Rue du Bac he had undertaken a charge almost equal to the three others. This was the Catholic Association of St. Francis of Sales, a work which sprang from the very heart of Pius the Ninth, and of which, notwithstanding his humble protestations to the contrary, Mgr. de Ségur must be regarded as the true founder. It was in 1856 that Mgr. de Mermillod and Père d'Alzon, the Superior of the Fathers of the Assumption, called the attention of the Holy Father to the danger menacing the faith of thousands from the proselytism of Protestant sects and the machinations of secret societies, and Pius the Ninth expressed his strong desire to see formed a great association of faith, prayer and alms, which should be, as he said, "a kind of Home Propaganda." Immediately on their return to Paris, Mgr. de Mermillod and Père d'Alzon called on Mgr. de Ségur to ask him to allow a meeting to be held in his *salon* for the purpose of consulting on the best means of realizing the Pope's idea.   He consented, and on the feast of St. Joseph, 1857, a very remarkable assembly of influential Catholics was gathered togetber in the Rue du Bac —Père Lacordaire, the Pères de Ravignan, Olivaint, and Ponlevoy, Père Ratisbonne, MM. Hamon, Desgenette and Deguerry, the venerated curés of Saint-Sulpice, N.D. des Victoires, and the Madeleine, were amongst the religious and secular priests present ; while conspicuous in the ranks of the laity were Montalembert, Louis Veuillot, the Vicomte de Melun, and Augustin Cochin.   A very simple body of statutes was drawn up, the *œuvre* placed under the patronage of St. Francis of Sales, and Mgr. de Ségur declared President, in spite of his representations that he had already more than he could manage.   However, he had to submit ; and as usual, set to work as though he had nothing else to attend to.   The Bishops hastened to send their cordial approval and promises of cooperation.   The good work was fairly started, the Père d'Alzon being, said Mgr. de Ségur " the true founder," a statement to which we must demur, for the Marquis's account plainly shows that the honour of the foundation is due to his saintly brother, who certainly had all the labour of it.   As a matter of fact, the meeting was called for the purpose of explaining the Pope's views, not of organizing the association.   All were unanimous in entrusting this onerous task to "the blind saint," and in ardently desiring its success :

but the majority, it seemed, were far from sanguine as to the result. As to the good Father whom Mgr. de Ségur insisted on calling the "founder," he appears, we must own, to have left the President in the lurch. Mgr. de Ségur says himself that after a few months Père d'Alzon left him "to settle matters as best he could"—*Se débrouiller de son mieux.*

And how did he succeed? The question even now, can only be answered by saying that God gave him extraordinary and special assistance. Before the end of the year the work had numbered several thousand associates and received more than thirty thousand francs, which were applied to founding schools, distributing good books, giving missions, and repairing or supplying with necessaries poor and neglected churches. As to Mgr. de Ségur's organization and management, one fact speaks volumes— twenty-four years later, at his death, there was nothing to alter, or correct, or improve. Everything was the same as at the beginning, except that instead of being established in forty dioceses, it was so in every diocese in France and in many in Belgium, Italy, Spain and Canada; that the number of associates was one million five hundred thousand, and the amount distributed yearly, eight hundred thousand francs. Think what these figures represent—the souls saved, the children taught, the sanctuaries restored! Think, too, of the labours, the self-sacrifice, which purchased these blessed results. With unwearied patience and perseverance he sought

for the right persons to be employed in the mani-
fold branches of the work; it was his rule that
every one engaged in working for God and the
Church, from the highest to the lowest, should be,
in the fullest sense *men of faith*, and we cannot
doubt that to the strict and invariable application
of this principle is due in great measure the constant and increasing success of the Association of
St. Francis of Sales, surely one of the greatest and
most singularly blessed even in France, fruitful as
she has ever been of such works for the glory
of God.

One of the heaviest charges imposed on him by
his new duties was that of preaching the object of
the *œuvre* in different parts of France. Fain would
we dwell on this part of his apostolic labours at
greater length, but we must content ourselves with
a few details of his visit to Annecy in 1865, when he
embraced the opportunity of the bi-centenary of the
canonization of St. Francis of Sales to preach the
work placed under his patronage in the very spot
sanctified by his relics. These were exposed for the
veneration of the faithful for some days before being
translated to the spot chosen by the saint for their
final resting-place, and from all the parishes, far and
near, processions, led by the curés, came flocking into
Annecy. The Bishop had begged Mgr. de Ségur to
receive these good souls and say a few words to them;
it was just what he delighted in : "while Mgr. de
Mermillod preached the great sermons, requiring

eloquence, I preached the little ones," he said. For
hours he remained, sitting or standing near the shrine,
and as each little band of pilgrims gathered round it,
he spoke to them for a few minutes, with his own
charming familiarity and grace, of some passage in
the saint's life, some virtue which he especially loved
and practised. From time to time came processions
entirely formed of children from the schools and
orphanages: then, indeed, he was in his element;
it might have been St. Francis himself teaching
these dear children of the poor the love of suffering
for the love of Christ, going into the details of their
simple lives and shewing them how to offer up to
their Lord reproofs and punishment, the heat which
tired them, the cold which pinched their little feet
and hands; and all because it was the will of God.
One most touching incident occurred, showing how
quickly one of these innocent souls responded to the
heroic teaching of the prelate for whom that holy
Will had chosen the same cross as for the little
Savoyard peasant. A poor woman, who had brought
her blind child to the shrine during one of Mgr. de
Ségur's addresses, said at its conclusion: "Now,
darling, ask our dear Saint to beg the good God to
give you your sight." "Oh mother," was the
answer, "did not you hear the priest say we must
wish nothing but the will of God? I am not going
to pray for my eyes, but for that."

CHAPTER VII.

Mission-work and Trials.

Out of the great Catholic Association of which some account was given in the last chapter arose a work, which, although its existence was, from a variety of causes, limited to a very few years, cannot be passed over in this sketch, as it was of Mgr. de Ségur's creation and very dear to him; its results, too, were solid and encouraging. Its object was to do for the spiritually destitute in the crowded *faubourgs* of Paris what St. Vincent of Paul had done, two centuries earlier, for those oppressed by corporal sufferings. The field was so vast: the population of these districts being more numerous than that of the whole of Paris in the reign of Louis the Sixteenth. Mgr. de Ségur's idea was to collect together those priests who were without parochial charge, and whose occupations, such as those of chaplains to religious communities and tutors in wealthy families, left them some leisure time which might be most profitably devoted to the work he was meditating. Conferences were to be held for organizing the plan and assigning to the different priests the missions desired by the Curés of parishes, and each meeting was to conclude by a familiar discourse from one of the members on a subject decided on at the preceding conference, which was to be a kind of exercise for the missionaries in the way of addressing their future hearers.

Mgr. de Ségur first consulted several of the most pious and experienced Curés of Paris, from whom he received advice and encouragement. Next, he ascertained that there were plenty of priests able and willing to work with him, there were not a few, even, among the *vicaires* of the richer parishes, who came forward and offered to give their evenings to the proposed work. He then laid his scheme before Cardinal Morlot, who bestowed on it his hearty approbation and earnest benediction, and on the feast of SS. Peter and Paul, 1858, the first conference was held, followed in a few weeks by the first mission in the Faubourg Saint-Jacques, which succeeded even beyond the expectations of Mgr. de Ségur's eminently hopeful mind. His rule and practice was to " preach the big truths (*les grosses vérités*) of the Catechism." Preachers often made a mistake, he used to say, in taking for granted that their hearers knew a great deal of which they are in reality profoundly ignorant: the same truths must be preached to shoeblacks and to senators.

Everywhere a plentiful harvest of souls rewarded the labours of the missionaries. The venerable Curé of Saint Louis-en-l'Ile—he was nearly a hundred years old—told them with tears that they

had "brought new life into his parish," and after a
Lent mission in another district, there were a
thousand more Easter Communions than in former
years. The Marquis gives a graphic account of the
mission at Ménilmontant, where, through the
negligence of the Government, there was only one
church, which could hardly, contain a thousand
persons, for a population of thirty thousand. These
poor people came in such crowds that it was necessary to station *gendarmes* at the doors to keep order ;
the sanctuary was filled with men in blouses up to
the altar-steps, and confessions went on till midnight. Numbers of poor abandoned women and
sinners of every kind were brought back to God, and
not knowing how to show their gratitude to those
who had converted them, they arranged and exhibited a grand show of fireworks in their honour
on the last day of the mission. The work was,
indeed, singularly blessed ; there were large workshops from which every man employed, the master
at their head, approached the sacraments after a
lifetime of neglect, and crowds of grown-up and
some aged persons made their First Communion.
One poor woman full of joy and thankfulness at
being reconciled with God, came a few days before
the close of the mission to the priest who had heard
her confession. "Ah, M. l'Abbé, how happy I am !
Now, if only you could get hold of my husband ! he
is a good fellow, but he will not hear of attending to
his soul. And yet he comes almost every day to

the mission;" and she went on to describe his appearance and the part of the church he occupied. " Now, do try to get at him ; he really isn't a bad sort, perhaps he might be caught ! Only be sure not to let him know I have been to confession, he would be ready to kill me !" Next day a workman with a huge beard, which was one of the "points" of the man in question, came to confession, and when he had received absolution said : " You see, M. l'Abbé, I have got a wife, not at all a pious woman—quite the other way ! Now, couldn't you manage to get her here ? I shall try to make sóme excuse to bring her here to-morrow. Only, pray don't tell her what I have been doing ; she would make game of me !" Of course the truth came out next day, and the good priest "chaffed" both his penitents for being " such a couple of geese as not to trust each other," sending them away very happy with a crucifix, a statue of our Lady, and two prayer-books.

Mgr. de Ségur always closed the missions by giving the Papal Benediction with the Plenary Indulgence, a favour granted to him by Pius the Ninth for all his missions and retreats. He made the ceremony as striking as possible, and the poor inhabitants of the faubourgs, who had never witnessed it before, were deeply impressed. " When we left the church," says the Abbé Diringer, " every one wanted to see ' the blind bishop,' and it was a difficulty sometimes to get through the crowd to the

carriage ; the said carriage being a humble hired
affair, the driver of which never missed Mgr. de
Ségur's instruction and benediction, always finding
some one to mind his horse, and nothing ever went
wrong in consequence."

It is not very clear from what cause this excellent
œuvre des faubourgs came to an end, certainly not
from any want of sympathy on the part of the good
Cardinal Morlot, who had encouraged it to the
utmost from the first. Mgr. de Ségur always felt
that it would have been an immense gain if the
Archbishop's enormous occupations could have
allowed of his coming, from time to time, among
these poor members of his flock, who are quite as
ready to be turned the right way as the wrong ; if,
as Augustin Cochin once suggested, there had been
stated times for his going to Notre Dame to receive
deputations from the different trades on their
patron's feast, to address them and give them his
blessing. " Who knows," asks the Marquis de
Ségur, "but that the horrors of the Commune might
thus have been prevented, and that even in the
moment of the wildest excitement, kindled for their
own ends by a few great criminals, the mass of the
people might not have been reacted upon by the
influence of religion and gratitude ? "

It has been seen that from the first Mgr. de Ségur
was convinced that his blindness was incurable,
and that he had mapped out his life entirely with
reference to its permanence. He never could bring

himself to ask or even to desire anything else, so that the visits which he made to the most celebrated oculists of Paris, in deference to the wishes of his family, must be regarded in the light of so many acts of resignation. He even yielded so far to his mother's wishes as to submit to an operation at the hands of M. Nélaton, who, contrary to all the other authorities who had been consulted, declared the case to be a simple cataract removable by operation. When this failed, the blow to the poor mother was severe; the sufferer himself had never expected any other result, and he hoped that those he loved would no longer cherish any idea of recovery. As to human means, they had indeed abandoned all hope; but could not God, if He so pleased, work a miracle for His servant? It was proposed to visit M. Dupont, and try the effect of the oil in the lamp which he kept burning night and day before the picture of the Holy Face, and by which so many wonderful cures had been obtained. Mgr. de Ségur had already paid one visit to the " holy man of Tours," and it seemed to him that, directly his eyes had been anointed by the latter, he saw, in one lightning flash, the Holy Face before which he knelt. He described it most exactly to his mother, and it is no wonder that, though the vision of an instant was followed by total darkness, she should have hoped much from a second visit. As usual, his mother's wish prevailed, and he consented with his own joyous serenity of manner.

But what had his prayer been on that first occasion, the prayer answered, if we may say so, by the momentary sight of his Master's blood-stained, thorn-crowned Face? It had been the prayer which was ever on his lips and in his heart, the prayer of his Divine Lord, that the Father's Will might be done; and while consenting to make a second visit to Tours, it was with a resolution to make no other petition. M. Dupont ventured on a remonstrance, writing to him that it is scarcely reasonable to expect a corporal favour unless it is asked for clearly and definitely, as the blind man asked in the Gospel, *Domine, ut videam.* It was in vain; he would only say, *Fiat Voluntas Tua* and the Father's answer was the continuance of the night, which was to last till the eternal day should break and bid "the shadows retire."

Once more he yielded to the longings of those who loved him, and visited the saintly Curé d'Ars. His prayers did not gain the grace they desired; but for both these great servants of God the meeting must have been full of consolation. Mgr. de Ségur knelt for the Curé's blessing, who in vain represented that it ought to be the other way; the blind prelate conquered at length in the contest of humility, by alleging the reverence due to M. Vianney's white hairs. They were soon engaged in conversation on the subjects dearest to both, and it was some time before Mgr. de Ségur remembered to speak of his mother's wishes. When he was about to take his leave, the Curé d'Ars took from the mantel-piece a little statue of St. John the Baptist, which he gave to Méthol, saying; " Here, my son, keep the image of your patron, as a remembrance of me."

Méthol's name was Jean-Baptiste, but Mgr. de Ségur never called him by it, and this was the first time that the holy curé ever saw him. After his visitor had left, M. Vianney said; " That blind man sees better than we do ;" and later on in the day he addressed a friend whom he met with the words ; " I have just seen a saint ;" words which may well be remembered as coming from the lips of one who read the hearts of men like a book.

So it was a fact to be accepted by all others now as well as by himself, that the cross was to be borne to the end of his life. And surely he was right in regarding his blindness as a greater blessing than a cure could have been, not only as regarded the work of his own sanctification, but also the good of souls, " Had he recovered his sight," says his brother, " he would have been made a bishop, and the good he did would have been local; it is to be doubted, too, whether he possessed the qualities of an administrator, so necessary for a perfect bishop ; whereas, in his state of blindness, his activity and success in the service of the Church were incomparable, . . . sowing broadcast good doctrine, good books, and Catholic traditions, evangelizing and sanctifying numbers of seminaries, giving to or training for the Church a store of holy priests to carry on the work of his apostolate.

Again, from a closer point of view, Mgr. de Ségur's blindness was a means of attracting and converting sinners, not only by the serenity with which he bore the trial, but by the way it helped those penitents who shrank, ashamed, from meeting the eye of the confessor, not knowing, poor souls, how wide is the mercy and how tender the compassion of the minister of Jesus Christ, a mercy and compassion which increase in proportion to the number and heinousness of the sins of his penitents." Once, when preaching a retreat at the University of Lille, and exhorting the students to confession, he said, " Come now; if there are any of you who are a little unwilling and ashamed to open your hearts to a priest, see how convenient it will be to do so to me who am blind and so cannot see you ! "

In 1858, Mgr. de Ségur's much-loved sister, Sabine, entered religion, and thenceforth some of his happiest moments were spent in the little parlour of the Visitation Convent. He often said Mass in the Chapel, and after his thanksgiving breakfasted in the parlour while his sister talked with him on the other side of the grille. His relations with the Community were very close and affectionate ; he gave them conferences in Lent, and frequently clothed and professed the religious, who always welcomed him as a true father, while the tie between himself and the sister, whose guide, friend, and confidant he had ever been, was only drawn closer since she gave herself to God.

Every year brought some new work to this

unwearied labourer in the vineyard. He became president of a little *œuvre*, which made very small show, but was in reality great from the love of the Blessed Sacrament which was its origin and spirit ; that for the providing and keeping up of sanctuary lamps. The rule of the Roman Ritual on this point had been strangely neglected of late years in France, especially in country parishes, and it was to restore its observance that Mlle. de Mauroy, a great friend of Pius the Ninth, set on foot the Association which, under the direction of Mgr. de Ségur and M. Hamon, the zealous curé of Saint-Sulpice, entirely removed from France the reproach of so flagrant a disrespect to the Blessed Sacrament. At the death of Mgr. de Ségur not only had more than four thousand lamps been given to poor churches and chapels, but more than thirty thousand asso-ciates were enrolled, who succeeded each other in making an hour of adoration before the Blessed Sacrament, placing themselves in spirit in the church nearest to them.

The four years which followed his sister's religious vocation were passed in the active and incessant labours entailed by all these various apostolic works, especially that of the evangelization of the *faubourgs* of Paris. At the end of this period Mgr. de Ségur, having lost his excellent father, consecrated to God a large portion of his inheritance by restoring and beautifying the parish church of Aube, endeared to him, as we have seen, by so many sacred asso-

J

ciations, and now made, by his reverent love, one of the most beautiful country churches of the diocese.

The year of his father's death, 1863, was marked by one of the severest blows which can befall a priest, the heavier, in this instance, from being entirely unexpected. A day or two before the Immaculate Conception, when his time was occupied from morning till night in hearing confessions, one of his regular penitents, whom he loved as a son, threw himself at his feet in an agony of remorse and poured into his ears a terrible story. He and four others, yielding to one of those strange and frightful temptations which proceed directly from the father of evil, had sworn to profane the Blessed Sacrament by committing sacrilege. No sooner was the sin accomplished than the wretched boy was horror-struck at his act and rushed to the chapel to confess it. Mgr. de Ségur, suppressing every sign of all he felt, and without uttering a word of reproach (it is of course, from the penitent himself that all this was learnt), gave him absolution, imposing on him no other penance than that of one " Hail Mary." The trembling boy, almost terrified at this calmness and indulgence, could not help crying out: "Oh, father! only that ? "

" Only that ; " was the grave sad answer. " Go in peace and sin no more. I take the rest on myself." And how was this promise kept ? First, with the consent of his poor young penitent, he

sent for the companions of his guilt, brought them
to a repentant state, and reconciled them to God.
Then, in spite of his limited means and the vast
claims upon him, he had *five thousand Masses of
expiation* said; he felt that no claim could equal
that of his Divine and outraged Lord, and that all
else must yield to the necessity of offering to Him
the only reparation equal to the offence. From
that day he bound himself to rise every night and
spend one or two hours before the Blessed Sacrament: and in order to do this without having to
rouse his faithful Méthol, he begged from the Abbot
of La Trappe at Mortagne, near Les Nouettes, a
large white Trappist's cowl, in which he could
easily wrap himself without assistance. The good
Abbot begged him to accept his own; and thus
habited, Mgr. de Ségur for fifteen years made his
vigil of expiation. If he ever missed doing so, it
was to go out with his servant, instead of retiring
to rest, to visit some one grievously sick, to pray
beside some corpse, to console some mourner:
works of mercy which—need it be said ?—were also
offered as acts of reparation. Then, calmly and
with absolute submission, he waited for the justice
of God to visit him.

A year had passed, and the feast of the Immaculate Conception was approaching. It almost seemed
as though God had chosen the anniversary of the
sacrilege for a solemn acceptance of His servant's
offering of himself in reparation. The dignity and

delicacy of the manner in which this distressing passage in his life is related by his brother is beyond all praise.   He prefaces the account by expressing the utmost respect for Mgr. Darboy, the greatest admiration for his heroic conduct in remaining at his post when the Government, headed by M. Thiers, fled before the Commune, his meekly-borne captivity, his death, which, like that of his predecessor, may well be called a martyrdom.   He excuses the harshness of the Archbishop to Mgr. de Ségur by generously admitting that he thought himself obliged to be severe in the defence of his office, and then, calmly and temperately, he tells his tale.

Mgr. de Ségur was aware that his views differed widely, in many important particulars, from the Archbishop's, and that the latter was fretted by the exceptional position occupied in his diocese by one of the leaders of " Ultramontanism ; " and it is fair to conclude, with the Marquis, that Mgr. Darboy was determined to take a step which should impress on the people of Paris that Mgr. de Ségur was entirely dependent on him.   Accordingly, when his authorization was requested for solemnizing a marriage in the chapel of the Rue du Bac, he refused it, and went on to speak with great bitterness of an interview between the Pope and Mgr. de Ségur, in which, he said, the latter made calumnious accusations against himself and other bishops.

In speaking of the painful scene, the blind Prelate regretted that, in the surprise and shock of this unexpected attack, he failed to meet it in the only way which could have protected him, that is, by replying that the interview had been confidential, and that what had passed was therefore the secret of the Holy Father. Instead of this, he eagerly disclaimed all intention of disrespect, declared much that had been reported to be inaccurate, and begged the Archbishop to observe that the subject of the interview had been the liberal and Gallican opinions of which he made no secret. Mgr. Darboy replied that as his information came from Rome, to deny its accuracy was to call in question the veracity of either His Holiness or Cardinal Antonelli. "Pardon me, monseigneur," was the calm answer, "it is possible to be mistaken without being false." In conclusion the Archbishop said that he required from him a declaration making full amends for the wrong he and his colleagues had suffered.

The question was: how to do this? and Mgr. de Ségur could not see his way. He waited some weeks, and then, as nothing further transpired, he began to hope that the Archbishop would be satisfied with the sharp reprimand he had given. Then came a letter threatening him with suspension unless a satisfactory declaration in writing were received in three days. Mgr. de Ségur consulted the Bishop of Poitiers, who unhesitatingly advised his yielding to the requirements of the Archbishop to the utmost extent possible, and accordingly he sent in an act of submission which he hoped would be deemed suffi-

cient. In the evening, he was hearing confessions at
the Collége Stanislas. The Abbé Diringer arrived
with a letter from the Archbishop, forbidding
Mgr. de Ségur to preach or hear confessions in his
diocese. There was a moment's silence ; then
falling on his knees before the Crucifix in the
sacristy he made the sacrifice of his interrupted
labours, of his injured honour. He asked the
Superior of the College to tell the boys he was
obliged to leave and nothing more, and on returning
home, quietly told his household what had happened : " St. Philip Neri," he said, " was suspended
for six years by the Pope ; now it is only my
Archbishop who has suspended me, so I cannot
complain." Then, going into the chapel with
them, he bade them join him in reciting, before the
Blessed Sacrament, some prayers suited to the
occasion. The first he chose was the *Magnificat.*
" We will recite it," he said, " to thank our Blessed
Lady for sending us this great opportunity of
sanctification."

All Mgr. de Ségur's friends felt how urgent it was
to bring about at any cost an accommodation of
what threatened to be a great scandal. M. Lalanne,
the excellent Superior of the Collége Stanislas, and
a venerable Canon, who was highly respected by
the Archbishop, called on Mgr. de Ségur to beg
him to make every possible concession to satisfy
Mgr. Darboy, who, they assured him, was very
anxious to retract the step which he had conceived

himself obliged to take. This good old priest had ventured, with the authority bestowed on him by his great age, to say to the Archbishop: "Monseigneur, is it possible that you have suspended the holiest priest in your diocese?" To which Mgr. Darboy replied without a sign of displeasure: "He has failed in his duty to me, and he owes me an apology." Needless to say that Mgr. de Ségur was ready to do his part: "I will do," he said, "with the help of God, whatever I can without injury to my office." Another declaration, fuller and more explicit than the former one, was drawn up and signed, with which Mgr. Darboy expressed himself satisfied, and thus, thanks to the humility of Mgr. de Ségur and the generosity of the Archbishop, this painful affair was settled.

It had produced more excitement in Rome than Paris, and the Pope certainly seems to have felt very strongly on the subject, as appears by a letter which Mgr. de Ségur's biographer wrote to his brother, and from which the following is an extract.

My dear Gaston,—I must tell you at once of the great favour I have just received from the Pope, and which certainly is due to you. Prince Borghese had proposed my taking Pierre (his younger brother) to the Holy Father's Mass, so I wrote yesterday to Mgr. Pacca, asking the Pope for this honour. . . . Yesterday morning we heard his Mass, received Holy Communion from him, and were about to withdraw, after hearing a second Mass in thanksgiving, when we received a message from the Pope that he wished to see us. We were shown into his study, in which five places were prepared at the breakfast-table ... so we breakfasted with him, talking to him just as one would to one's father. . . . He spoke of you at once, saying: 'So your brother's business is settled—that is all over;' then he said in Italian to Prince Borghese: 'That affair has not ended in the way I should have liked: when any-thing is said to the Pope, it is a secret which belongs only to the Pope.' I said: 'Holy Father, I must warn your Holiness that I understand what you say.' He laughed and said: 'There—it is over—we will say no more about it. It can't be helped, your brother is a saint!' I think, as the Prince said when we went away, that was a grand thing to hear from the lips of him who canonizes the saints. You see, then, my dear Gaston, that the Pope considers your fault to have been an excess of virtue, and I feel what he said of you to be a very great consolation. It is plain that this rare favour of receiving me at his own table was his charming and fatherly way of making known, first to you, then to all the world, his opinion of your affair. . . . I have not had anything about it put in the papers. I just leave the thing, for I do not think it is for me to take anything upon myself in one sense or another, knowing, as I do, that the honour done me by the Pope goes far beyond me and is intended for others. As we left the Vatican, Prince Borghese said that he and I have to thank you for the honour: it is as clear as daylight : *Qui se humiliat exaltabitur.*

Thus God answered His servant's prayer: it was

a terrible trial, though a short one, the special sting being in the hand by which the blow was dealt. He told his most intimate friends that each succeeding year, towards the feast of the Immaculate Conception, God sent him some particular trial to remind him of the sacrilege of 1863 and the expiation he had promised. The reminder of 1869 was a very sharp one. It was on the feast itself, the first day of the Vatican Council, a day which he had desired so ardently and hailed so hopefully. On that very morning, his name was posted at the door of St. Peter's, in the sight of all the bishops of the Christian world, between the names of Dr. Döllinger and the unhappy Père Hyacinthe. By some strange accident, in spite of the holiness of the writer and the particular affection borne to him by the Pope, the Italian translation of one of his treatises had been placed on the *Index*, without giving him the opportunity of explanation or correction. A Bishop who was a great friend of his, writing to him on the subject, said : " Seeing you in such company made me think of our Lord between two thieves."

It was, as the Marquis says, a blow to his honour as a Catholic writer, as the suspension five years before had been to his honour as a priest. He always submitted his works to be examined by good theologians before publishing them, and he was utterly unprepared for their being found assailable in any point. He knew indeed that in a dogmatic treatise a very small error is sufficient to place it on the *Index* : still the blow was a very severe one, and he said that but for God's support he felt as if it would turn his brain. The very day on which the news reached him he sent a public submission, full of exquisite humility, to the *Univers*, and instantly suppressed the whole of the French edition of his treatise, (though it was the Italian translation only which had been condemned), and re-wrote it with great care. There can be no better commentary on this painful passage in Mgr. de Ségur's life than the eloquent passage from his funeral oration by Mgr. de .Mermillod, quoted by the Marquis de Ségur :

Henceforth, there was nothing lacking to his sa-cerdotal crown. Crucified in his body by blindness, humiliated in his priestly character by the suspension which ordinarily strikes unworthy or rebellious priests, in his reputation as an author by the condemnation of the Holy Roman Church of which he was the devoted son and champion, struck by his Archbishop and by the Pope in turn, he knew, like his Divine Master, the meaning of suffering. Thus, by accepting his covenant with the Cross, God let all men see how worthy he was to carry it, and that he had a right to preach it by his written and spoken word, because he preached it more eloquently still by his example.

CHAPTER VIII.

Labours for the sick and the army.

VERY high in the long list of Mgr. de Ségur's friends must be placed the sons of St. Francis of Assisi. Himself a Tertiary of his Order, he preached devotion to the great patriarch through the whole of his priestly life, and it was his great delight to spend a few days from time to time in the Monastery at Versailles. A few years before his death he cherished the hope of retiring altogether from the world with some other Tertiaries, and devoting himself exclusively to the evangelization of the working classes, and although he abandoned the idea in deference to those he consulted and who considered the step unadvisable, he always observed the rule of the Third Order, fasting three times a week as long as his health made this possible.

His relations with the Brothers of St. John of God were very close and affectionate. He visited their house in the Rue Oudinot very frequently, and sent them as patients many young men, students and others, knowing that they would find there physicians for the soul as well as for the body, and many of them were received by the good Brothers free of all charge.

Of this number was Pierre Sazy, an orphan of sixteen, whose story is very touching. He had been adopted by a Protestant aunt, who was incessantly urging him to abandon the Catholic faith, and who, after years of persecution, giving up the attempt as useless, turned him out of doors. The lad was apprenticed to a gilder, with whom he lodged and boarded during the week, but from Saturday to Monday he was homeless and destitute. For six successive Sundays this poor young confessor to the faith had been absolutely without a mouthful of food, and the nights, in bitter winter weather, had been spent in wandering about the streets. At length he providentially met a Sister of Charity who had nursed his mother in her last illness, and she took him to Mgr. de Ségur, who received him with open arms. Thenceforward his Sundays were spent in the Rue du Bac. What a paradise that house must have seemed to the poor waif of the Paris streets, with its wholesome food, comfortable bed, and the fatherly affection which welcomed him! But the earthly paradise was soon exchanged for the heavenly one; cold and hunger had done their work, and the doctor whom Mgr. de Ségur consulted pronounced Pierre to be in the last stage of consumption. He was taken to the Rue Oudinot, and received by the good religious as an angel from Heaven. Then followed three months of sufferings borne joyfully for God's sake, of daily Communions, of heavenly consolations, followed by a death so blessed that the Brothers spoke of it as a benediction for their house.

They had another at Vaugirard, known as the "house for incurable children," also frequently visited by Mgr. de Ségur, who was honorary president of the meetings of the lady patronesses, to whom, as well as to the children, he always addressed a few words. It was his aim to establish a *personal* feeling on both sides, and he induced many of the ladies, with excellent effect, to take a particular child under their especial patronage, whom they made it a duty to visit, encourage, and reward. Here is a pretty instance of what the Marquis calls, "the contagion of sanctity." Several of the children were blind, and these were naturally particularly noticed by Mgr. de Ségur. One of them, who was very unfortunate in stumbling against obstacles, sometimes gave himself severe blows, and once, after Mgr. de Ségur's death, he came to see the Abbé Diringer with the mark of a deep gash on his forehead. On being asked about it, he said: "Oh it is nothing. I ran up against a door, but I don't mind now, since Monseigneur gave me his prescription." "And what was it?" "Well, he said to me one day: Look here, my child; whenever we blind people give ourselves a knock, or get hurt in any way, all we have to do is just to say, My good Jesus, I thank You. Then it is all right. I took his advice, and ever since I have not troubled myself about such accidents: I thank God, and think no more about it."

The two years preceding the war brought many trials to Mgr. de Ségur. The first was the death of his beloved sister Sabine, which, in spite of the immense consolations which accompanied it, he always spoke of as his greatest sorrow, except the loss of his mother five years later. He had the first warning of that crowning grief about this time. Madame de Ségur had an apoplectic stroke, and was entirely given over by the doctor. Her son gave her the last sacraments, which she received with the utmost calmness and piety, and on being exhorted to trust in God and to banish all fear and anxiety, she answered simply : " I feel none. I quite hope that God will receive me in His mercy." Soon after, an old friend of the family arrived with some water from Lourdes ; Mgr. de Ségur put a few drops on the wet cloths which bandaged her head ; she at once fell quietly asleep and the next day was out of danger. A few months later he made a pilgrimage of thanksgiving to Lourdes, and thenceforward devotion to our Lady of Lourdes was a prominent feature of his spiritual life.

Not long after his sister's death he had to endure a trial of a very different kind. He had written a pamphlet on Freemasonry, in which, with a courage which some called rashness, he exposed many horrors of that " Mystery of evil," even going so far as to publish some secret documents communicated to him by perverted Catholics, who had afterwards repented and withdrawn from the society.

Articles in the journals of the sect insulted him, anonymous letters threatened his life, without ruffling his calmness in the slightest degree. One morning a stranger entered the chapel while he was saying Mass. Both M. Diringer and Méthol noticed his appearance as peculiar, there was a curious restlessness in his manner, and his eyes were hidden by blue spctacles. After making his thanksgiving, Mgr. de Ségur went into the next room to hear confessions, the stranger remaining in the chapel till the last. At length his turn came; Méthol, overpowered by some presentiment of evil, hid himself behind the *portière* with a knife in his hand. The man abruptly asked Mgr. de Ségur whether it was possible to be a Freemason and yet remain a Catholic? Startled by the question and the tone in which it was asked, Mgr. de Ségur rose, saying, "You are a Freemason, are you not? What are you here for?" His visitor replied that his object was to warn him that at a recent meeting his death was resolved, in consequence of his writings against secret societies. The blind prelate's answer was to throw his arms round the unhappy man saying, "Look what your Freemasonry is, which professes to be a benevolent society! No sooner is it accused, on irrefragable evidence, of revolutionary plans, than it replies by a threat of assassination!"

The man disengaged himself from Mgr. de Ségur's embrace, saying, "It may be all very true, but I am not here to argue. You once did a service to a relation of mine, and I came, out of gratitude, to give you this warning. Be on your guard, but tell no one what I have done, as it would very likely be my death." Mgr. de Ségur tried in vain to persuade the wretched man to break his accursed bonds; and he went away saying that he did not know when the decree of death was to be carried out, but that it would be before the opening of the Vatican Council. Mgr. de Ségur was fully convinced of the man's truthfulness, and making the sacrifice of his life he lived for some time as it were in the shadow of death. Nothing would have been easier than to carry out the threat, especially when we consider his blindness. His door was open to all, and in the discharge of his sacred ministry, he was of course continually alone with his visitors, but he changed none of his habits for a single day, and no anxiety or alarm for an instant ruffled his beautiful serenity. Méthol did, indeed, take upon himself now and then to refuse admittance to some visitor whose appearance seemed questionable. But as, after all, an intruding assassin would most probably have assumed a devout and edifying deportment, there was really nothing for it but to trust Divine Providence, and Méthol, who was on guard long after his master had forgotten the whole matter, was not at ease till after the opening of the Council.

An incident took place shortly after the warning just related, which seems, as the Marquis says, like a special mark of God's favour sent to console

His servant under accumulated trials. He was preaching the *œuvre* of St. Francis of Sales at Lorient, and one day when the sacristy of the Church was full of priests and laymen, a respectable woman made her way through the crowd leading by the hand her little nephew, about six years old, who had been quite blind for several months. The doctors could do nothing for him, and the most eminent among them gave it as his opinion that the only chance was an operation, and his mother had decided on taking him to Nantes for this purpose. The child's aunt was, however, bent on first taking him to Mgr. de Ségur. "I shall ask him to give Félix his blessing," she said, "and I am sure that then God will cure him." She made her request, and Mgr. de Ségur taking the boy in his arms, laid his hands on his eyes and blessed him solemnly. Next morning, when the aunt brought Félix his breakfast, and was preparing to feed him as usual, he said, "What are you doing, aunt? I can feed myself. I see you and everybody quite well." In fact, he was quite cured. The news spread quickly, and when Mgr. de Ségur, who was leaving Lorient that day, went to the station, he could hardly make his way through the crowd. He never mentioned the matter himself, and it was not till after his death that his family collected evidence on the subject.

The Vatican Council was opened; and Mgr. de Ségur, "debarred by his blindness from taking part

K

in its interior work, followed every phase of its discussions with intense interest. Everywhere and to all, by his writings and sermons and advice in the confessional, he preached the spirit of obedience, of humble cheerful submission to the authority of the Church ; he showed how puerile and unbecoming were the theological discussions which were turning the heads of so many young men in the press, in clubs, and *salons*. In every possible way, with unwearied arguments, and patient charity, he reiterated the old Catholic axiom of true faith and true humility : *Ubi Petrus, ibi Ecclesia*."

No sooner was the Papal Infallibility defined than the terrible Franco-Prussian war broke out. The Emperor Napoleon, like his uncle, had brought ruin on himself and his dynasty by a sacrilegious attack on the Vicar of Christ, and it is impossible, as the Marquis de Ségur says, not to see more than mere accident in the remarkable coincidences which he points out. The disaster at Reichsoffen befel on the anniversary of the desertion of Rome by the French army, the battle of Sedan was fought on the 2nd of September, the day of the meeting at Plombières and of the Emperor's fatal *Faites vite*. Paris was invested by the Prussians on the same day that Rome was invested by the Piedmontese troops, a day which was, moreover, the anniversary of Castelfidardo, and the eve of the apparition at La Salette when our Lady announced the misfortunes of France and Rome.

This year Mgr. de Ségur passed his holidays at his sister's residence, Kermadio, near Sainte-Anne-d'Auray, where their mother had also gone. No one thought then that the siege of Paris would last beyond a few weeks, and he for a time sharing these illusions, was very willing to await the issue in Brittany. The neighbourhood of Auray was a great attraction both from personal devotion, and from the opportunities it afforded of doing good among the poor *mobiles* who flocked to the shrine of *Madame Sainte Anne*, as they passed through Auray. These hopes for Paris were quickly dashed, still more so by the insane spirit which prevailed there than by the military disasters of which every day brought tidings. On Jannary 1, 1870, he writes to the young seminarians of Montmorillon : " What sort of year will this be which begins so mournfully under the heel of the Prussians, and the far more terrible hand of the godless Revolution ? Well, my children, if we choose to make it so, it will be a very good year in spite of all the demons without and within ; for the good years are not those in which we weep and suffer least, but those in which we merit most, and love God most. If, during this year, we sow all our minutes and hours, like so many grains of wheat, in the ever fruitful soil of the Kingdom of Heaven, then we shall have a very good year in spite of the devil and his companions, in spite of Bismarck and his savages, in spite of the Revolution and its sectaries. To wish you a different sort of year than that, would, I think, be wishing for what is impossible, for we are a very long way from being converted. . . . If we were threatened with the Prussian scourge only, if there were not these revolutionary atheists to deal with, there would be good reason to hope for a speedy deliverance, but Almighty God, in His terrible mercy, is striking us, so to speak, with both hands, and the hardest blows are yet to come."

These six months of war, the destruction of the Empire, the horrors of the Commune, had gradually drawn Mgr. de Ségur's thoughts more and more closely to the old traditions of the French monarchy; and, as usual, going straight to the point, he not only published a pamphlet setting forth his sentiments in the plainest manner, but as head of the family, wrote to the Comte de Chambord, to give his formal adhesion to his cause and the principle it embodied. There were some who feared that his influence as a priest might be weakened by this step; but it was not so. As his brother says, it was evident to most people that there was no alternative between the Republic and the old Monarchy, and Mgr. de Ségur's view was understood by every one.

The last months spent at Kermadio were full of work and activity. The railway which passes close to the château brought him an endless succession of penitents, *mobiles*, volunteers, and Charrette's Zouaves, who hastened to spend a few hours with ' the soldiers' friend," to be reconciled by him to

God, and to receive strength and consolation for the hard future. He visited Poitiers and Montmorillon, nominally for a little rest, but the work went on much as before. His secretary, the excellent Abbé Diringer, was much taken up with a ministry which must have been as fruitful of pain as of consolation, and most surely abounding in merit, full of grief as he was over the loss of his unhappy birth-place Alsace. Auray was at this time full of German prisoners, many of them Catholics, and he was indefatigable in hearing their confessions and giving them all the consolations of the faith, but the suffering to one who was " French and Alsatian from head to foot," was severe.

After the defeat of the Commune, Mgr. de Ségur went to Les Nouettes for the first Communion of one of his nieces, but before doing so he spent some weeks in Paris, where his presence was eagerly desired by the many souls who had been deprived of his ministry so long. It was a surprise and joy to find his rooms in the Rue du Bac, above all the chapel, "the place he loved most on earth," uninjured. He was prepared to find it a scene of desolation, and had made the sacrifice in anticipation. He used to say that times of public calamity and disturbance ought to detach us from many things. "They make us see and feel that things good and sweet and useful in themselves, things which seemed almost necessary, were after all only pleasant, and that we can do perfectly well without them,

Amongst these is our pretty devotional chapel ; so, too, our good little rules of life and fixed habits. . . All these things were very good; but there is something a great deal better, and that is full and perfect submission to the holy will of God."

A still deeper joy was that of finding by far the greater part of his dear Patronage children, apprentices and workmen, in excellent dispositions; of course there were exceptions, but he had the happiness of seeing those who had been drawn into the madness and sin of the time hasten with touching eagerness to pour out their hearts to their friend and father and be reconciled by him to the God they had offended. After a fortnight in Paris he returned to Normandy to preach a retreat to his nieces, who were making or renewing their First Communion. His mother, most of his brothers and sisters with their families were present; it was a family festival as well as a solemn Christian one. And it was for the last time ; neither his mother nor he ever saw the old home again.

On returning to Paris Mgr. de Ségur's labours were increased by two new *œuvres*, to which he devoted himself with all his usual enthusiasm and perseverance. The first was that known as the *Œuvre de l'Alsace-Lorraine*, in which his friendship for the Abbé Diringer gave him an additional interest. Whole families, on the Prussian annexation of the two provinces, quitted houses, country and occupations, rather than lose their French nationality. A committee, of relief, under the presidency of the Comte d'Haussonville, to which persons of every shade of opinion hastened to subscribe, was at once formed, but from the fact of its generality, it could not provide sufficiently for the religious wants of these poor people, so deeply and sincerely Catholic, whose faith was seriously endangered by the want of German-speaking priests, and whose morals were exposed to the contaminating influences of Parisian life. It was to supply this want that the *œuvre* in question was founded. Mgr. de Ségur continued to preside over it till his death, and it was blessed beyond all expectation. Special chaplains were appointed to districts inhabited by the emigrants, where catechisms, sermons, and retreats, were soon in full work : schools and orphanages were established, burses founded for placing apprentices and for enabling the young clerics expelled from the seminaries of Metz and Strasbourg to continue their studies. In the orphanage of Sens alone, admirably conducted by the Sisters of Providence, a hundred and fifty children of the *œuvre* have in ten years been trained and established in factories, houses of business, railways, post-offices, and telegraph-companies, while the number of families that have been relieved is beyond calculation. Let us add, in conclusion, that the committee have sent more than forty thousand francs to the African dioceses for the religious necessities of the colonists from Alsace and Lorraine.

The other work which we have referred to was
that concerning military chaplains. This little
sketch has shown how truly Gaston de Ségur
deserved his title of "the soldiers' friend," from
the days when he gave the first-fruits of his
ministry to the military prisons of Paris; it will be
remembered how the evangelization of the French
army of occupation had been his favourite work in
Rome, and now he was ready to "spend and be
spent," in the cause so dear to his heart. He regarded the religious and moral training of the
army, that is to say, of every young Frenchman in
turn, as the salvation of his country, the absolute
condition of her welfare. He had striven, before
the war broke out, for a regular legal organization
of the military chaplains; his efforts had been
fruitless, but at that time the Church still enjoyed
comparative liberty of action, and there were in
every garrison town voluntary chaplains chosen by
the bishops and accepted by the commanding officers.
When the war broke out there was no official system
for the religious wants of the army, and the
Government was taken by surprise here as in all
other matters. It was left to private charity to supply the deficiency, and from one end of France
to the other the work was nobly carried on. The
good that was done is not to be told; a few
plain facts will tell their own tale. Father
Ambrose, a Capuchin, says that during the
war he visited three thousand sick and wounded,

confessed a thousand, anointed nearly three hundred, and gave Holy Viaticum to about half that number ; if these figures are multiplied by two hundred and ten, the number of chaplains provided or assisted by Mgr. de Ségur's committee, it will give an idea of the work done for God and for souls.

In Paris and its environs, the results were, perhaps, still more striking, as they were not helped on by the powerful stimulus of imminent danger and approaching death, as on the scene of war. At Charenton, during a fortnight, the Abbé Courtade calculated that at least twenty-five hundred men made their confessions, and a Eudist Father, Père Féron, says that he and a colleague confessed whole regiments passing through Paris, and in one church alone nearly three thousand received Holy Communion. Neither were the dead forgotten ; and it was in a great measure owing to the assistance of Mgr. de Ségur's committee that the well-known Pere Joseph carried out his touching *œuvre* for erecting Christian monuments in all the German cemeteries where French prisoners lie, and for founding Masses for the repose of their souls.

But this was not all. Mgr. de Ségur laboured incessantly for the official establishment of the military chaplains. The matter was beset with difficulties ; several of the *députés*, though good Christians, and personally desirous of the success of the project, were restrained by timidity and human respect from committing themselves openly; and it may be safely said that the plan which was laid before the National Assembly, and which eventually passed into a law, owed its existence to the frequent meetings in the Rue du Bac, at which the most experienced of the voluntary chaplains and the *députés* who were heart and soul with Mgr. de Ségur in the matter held consultation. The law, when passed, left much to be desired; still, despite many shortcomings and omissions, it was a great gain, and the strongest proof of the good. it produced is the fact that one of the first steps of the declared Republican Government was its suppression. To quote the Marquis de Ségur: "It ' passed doing good,' like so many other Christian works which share in the life of the Divine Master, but it passed quickly, and Good Friday followed Palm Sunday. It was a sharp blow to Mgr. de Ségur, whose only consolation was in the hope of seeing Easter follow Good Friday."

Soon after the passing of this important law God sent His servant the great sorrow of his life, his mother's death. He used to speak of his love for her as " the one passion of his life," and certainly it was the great sorrow of his life when he held her in his arms in the chill dawn of that February morning, and she gave up her spirit to God just as he pronounced the Last Blessing. He went instantly to his chapel and offered up the Holy Sacrifice for her soul. While saying Mass his tears fell so fast and thick that the vestment he wore was soaked through, tears doubly touching, as his brother says, falling from sightless eyes.

He said the Requiem Mass on the day of her funeral, the Bishop of Poitiers giving the absolutions : after the ceremony the latter said to him the touching, often-quoted words, which lose so much by translation. *Mon ami, on devient vieux à partir du jour où l'on n'a plus sa mère*—" We begin to be old men the day we lose our mother."

The Marquis says that his brother's health visibly declined from the time of his mother's death : not only was the strongest tie which bound him to the earth broken, leaving a wound which never healed, but the labours which had been before all but incessant, were henceforth to know no interruption. The fortnight's rest which he had taken with his mother in the summer was abandoned, and he threw himself, if possible, with more devotion than ever into the multiplied works of his vast apostolate. One of these, which has not yet been mentioned, must be slightly sketched before concluding this chapter. At a congress of the directors of the various Workmen's Associations it was resolved to establish a Central Office which, without exercising any sort of authority over the different diocesan offices or *œuvres*, should serve as a link by means of which all should profit by the experience of the rest, and also provide at a reduced rate, books, articles of piety, games, and innumerable other

things for the Patronages.   Another important function of the Central office was that of fixing and
arranging for the annual congresses held first in
one episcopal city, then in another, which the
Marquis de Ségur well describes as "the assizes of
Catholic charity to the working classes."   Mgr. de
Ségur, who could refuse nothing which was asked
in the name of those so dear to him, accepted the
office of President.   It was represented to him as
a sort of sinecure, his name being all that was
wanted, and without relying absolutely on this
statement, he was not prepared for the amount of
labour, the overwhelming anxiety, entailed by his
new duties.   He presided for nearly eight years at
the fortnightly meetings, and on him, too, devolved
all the letters to the Pope, the Bishops, the
Superiors of the diocesan Seminaries, not to speak
of his articles in the *Bulletin* of the society, in which
appeared one of his most useful little works, *The
young Christian workman.*   Last, but far from least,
was the trying office of asking alms, his *croix
d'argent*, as he called it—the play upon the word is
untranslatable.

   When attacked for the first time by congestion of
the brain, in 1879, he wrote a letter to excuse his
absence from the congress at Angers, from which
we give the following beautiful passage :

   "Our Lord, Whose devoted servants we all of us
are, has sent me a little trial by which His will is made

very plain. And so, my dear friends, I cannot even say that I am sorry not to be able to share your labours, for we must love doing good works only because it is the expression of our Divine Master's will to us, and then, you know as well as I do, that, if it is good to labour for Him, it is better still to suffer for Him; and never did the Son of God labour so efficaciously for His Father's glory and for the good of souls, as when He hung silent and motionless on His Cross of anguish. That is the best place, believe me, and I am sure you will give me a proof of true Christian affection by thanking Jesus with me and for me. Only ask of Him for your old friend and servant sincere humility, constant sweetness, and the best of all medicines, the height of all perfection, patience. I will offer the Holy Sacrifice for you on the day the congress opens, and also on the next day, the 2nd of September, which is a great and sacred anniversary of mine—it will be twenty-five years on that day since I lost my sight, a grace for which I thank our Lord twenty-five thousand times. I venture to beg from you a special Communion of thanksgiving, that I may keep this ' silver wedding ' of my blindness more worthily with the Crucified and Merciful Jesus. And now, my dear and kind friends, go on working in a spirit of holiness for the true happiness and welfare of our poor people. Let the wicked abuse us—the disciple is not above His Master."

Two months after writing this letter, he resigned the office of President.

IX.

Last days.

MGR. DE SEGUR's health gradually declined from the time of his mother's death, but his first attack of congestion of the brain, his "first warning," as he called it, was not till five years later. The interval had brought him many trials, of which his failing health, was, perhaps, the least; the will of God had been so long and so constantly his rule and guide that he was as ready to be laid by "like a worn out tool," as to work in the vineyard; yet, even so, the interruptions which broke in now so often upon his apostolate, the necessity of restricting his labours and of taking rest must have been a cross. These five years, too, were marked by the deaths of many most dear to him. The charity of a Roman prelate, who had obtained his leave to pay the expenses of his journey to Rome and his stay there, procured him the consolation of standing by the death-bed of one of these, the grand old soldier Mgr. Bastide, who had been struck down by para-lysis of the brain. He recognized the "Gaston" whom he had loved so well, and thanked God for the joy of seeing him. We may well believe that he was allowed to receive the visit of another beloved friend, who had died some months before, and who seemed to have been sent to welcome him to Paradise. Just before he breathed his last, Mgr. Bastide suddenly regained the power of speech, his face lighted up, and he cried out two or three times in a strong voice, "Come, Mérode, come!" Three years later Mgr. de Ségur paid his last visit to Rome, to assist at the funeral of him who was to him Pope, father, friend, and guide. The Marquis, at this point of his biography, dwells at some length on the friendships of his brother, always an interesting page in the lives of the great and good, but over which we must not linger long. Three of his most intimate lay friends were Louis Veuillot, Auguste Nicolas, and Gounod. A few words may be given to the last of the trio. Mgr. de Ségur first met him at Rome; in Paris they soon became great friends. He delighted in Gounod's varied gifts, and used to say that besides being a great musician, the first lyrical composer of his time, a poet and a brilliant talker, he was "almost a theologian." Gounod opened his whole heart to his blind friend, his life had no secrets from him, sometimes he called him "father," sometimes "Gaston;" wherever they went, they talked long and intimately, and the conversation, however it began, was sure to get to Rome by some way or other. Even in the closing days of Mgr. de Ségur's life, when his soul was sometimes overshadowed by his bodily sufferings,

Gounod was always able to brighten him up, and, as the Marquis says, to " call forth the hearty laugh of an innocent soul, that touching joyous laugh of children and of priests." This holy and beautiful friendship was an inspiration under the influence of which some of Gounod's loveliest *cantiques* were composed, as well as " Polyeucte " and the " Rédemption." A very few months before Mgr. de Ségur's death, he begged him to come once more to dine *en famille* with him, his wife and his children. After dinner he took him into his study, which is quite a sanctuary, having at one end a splendid organ, and, for its chief ornament a striking head of our Lord by Franceschi. Here he played and sang to him some of the finest passages of that religious work (the " Rédemption," the words of which (also Gounod's) are as full of inspiration as the music, and Mgr. de Ségur sat and listened, as it were, to the echoes of the heavenly strains he was soon to hear in Paradise."

Next to the friendship of Pius the Ninth, the greatest honour and one of the greatest joys of Mgr. de Ségur's life was the strong and faithful attachment of the illustrious Bishop of Poitiers, whose death preceded his own by a year. It was a great blow to him, and, notwithstanding his broken health, he undertook the journey to Poitiers to assist at the funeral of his friend, the " Hilary of the nineteenth century," as Mgr. Pie has been aptly named.

The first attack of congestion of the brain was not severe in itself, but very serious as regards the future, and he was ordered entire rest in the country; he went at once to his sister's château in Brittany to spend the next two or three months "like a Catholic oyster," as he said, hoping at the end of that time to begin work again gradually; but henceforth his whole life was an immediate preparation for death. Like St. Francis of Sales he was continually "on the alert," but far from losing any of his cheerfulness in consequence, his gentle constant gaiety seemed only to brighten as the "perfect day" drew near. He wrote to a religious of the Assumption, who was his spiritual daughter: "It is a little warning from the doorkeeper of Paradise, St. Peter, to get my packing done. Now I expect you to help me in this, like a true Sister of Charity: women, especially Sisters, understand the business better than men do. So I leave it to you, my dear Sister, and to your holy companions." He writes to Dom Gréa from Kermadio: "Here we are, the Abbé Diringer and I, in absolute solitude, on the land of Sainte-Anne-d'Auray, where it is so quiet that you can hear the flies' wings; and here we mean, please God, to remain till October, without moving, or seeing anybody, or making any visits except to the Blessed Sacrament, in a pretty new Breton church, twenty minutes off, where there is the best curé in the world and an excellent *vicaire*. On the way there, very near to us, rests my dear

L

mother, to whom we also pay a visit as we go or return. I hope to continue, as I have begun, to say Mass in a little impromptu chapel. We only mean to do just enough work to prevent our feeling dull, and we shall live a good deal in the open air, trying, too, to live very faithfully and calmly, from day to day, from hour to hour, as our Lord bids us do."

The quiet life in Brittany had good results, the brain was calm, the speech much clearer; and he thus announces the improvement and his hopes of doing a little work, in one of his letters: "I am much better; and when I begin, very gradually, to do some work again for souls, I shall soon see whether our dear Lord and Master means to put me on one side, like an old soldier whose time of service is up, or whether, in His goodness, He still intends to make use of me to sweep consciences, or to do washing, rough or fine, or to mend broken pots, or to act as gardener or servant of some sort, no matter what I am called or what my wages are."

Preaching was impossible, on account of his speech being still, though not seriously, affected: he heard confessions, as usual, except in the evenings, without appearing to suffer; and in the February of 1880, he celebrated two marriages in his family. So the months went on, till a second seizure occurred just after the Assumption. It was not more severe than the first, but it was another stage of the last journey. His manner of life continued as before, and he was even able to work a little every day at a book on the most striking miracles at Lourdes, in which he was intensely interested, his last tribute of devotion to the Immaculate Mother of God. On the 18th of December, he writes to the religious of whom we have just spoken: "This morning, my dear Sister, I celebrated the thirty-third anniversary of my first Mass, and I think I did so with a deeper sense of happiness than ever. And yet, as one grows old, and feels more and more the burden of age and infirmity, devotional feelings droop and become slow and difficult. It is a condition to which I was a stranger till I had my little attack last year, and I find it very dreary and depressing. You must beg our dear Lord to enable me to profit by this share in the grace of the beginning of His Agony: "He began to grow sorrowful and to be sad."

It was on Good Friday, the 15th of April, his sixty-second birthday, that Mgr. de Ségur had a third, and more serious attack. With a submission so prompt, that it seemed to cost him nothing, he made the sacrifice of his labours for the close of Holy Week, and soon after Easter he left Paris for his second brother's house, at Méry. After a short stay he returned to the Rue du Bac; he had invited his little incurables to come to Mass in his chapel, and on May 28, 1881, it was full of "the poor and the feeble and the blind and the lame;" there were paralyzed children who had to be laid before the altar, and it was in the midst of these sufferers, so dear to the Sacred Heart and to his own, that this father of the poor said his last Mass. He could hardly get through it; it was with great difficulty that he genuflected, and he often leant upon the altar to support himself in a standing posture, yet after his thanksgiving he went into the dining-room where a little feast was prepared for the children, and helped his secretary and Méthol to wait on them. Never had he been more fatherly or more bright and cheerful, and when he retired to rest he appeared much as usual, but before morning he was taken seriously ill. His doctor insisted on his being removed from the little cell which was his sleeping-chamber, and from the bed which the poorest patient in a hospital would have refused. It was, in fact, one small hard mattrass laid on the top of a rough chest. After some search, an old iron bedstead was discovered in the loft, this was moved into the *salon* and covered with a couple of borrowed mattrasses, and on it he passed the ten days he had to spend on earth. There were many alternations of hope and fear before the former was quite abandoned. There was continued dulness and torpor of the brain unless he was spoken to, and then he always replied promptly and with his usual gracious sweetness. Sometimes, for hours together, he imagined himself in the confessional, and the watcher by his side would see his hand raised continually to make the sign of the Cross, and hear the broken voice whisper: "Say three Hail Marys for your penance."

Once he thought he was at Lourdes, and could hardly believe it was not so; he said to his brother in the morning: "Well, they say that I have not really been at Lourdes just now, so I must believe them, but it is difficult to think it was fancy."

Everywhere, not in France only, but throughout the Catholic world, prayers, Masses and Communions were offered for his cure. For some days, only his nearest relatives were admitted to his room; and, as at his mother's death, all his brothers and sisters, except one who was on a sick bed, were in Paris. On the feast of Pentecost, the oppression of his chest increased so much that, though he was not suffering pain, it was thought well to anoint him. He consented joyfully, making all the responses himself, and repeating, again and again afterwards, "How beautiful it all is! how good it is!"

And now that those who loved him best saw clearly that it was not God's will to keep him longer with them, they felt that this deathbed of an apostle must not be regarded as an ordinary one, his countless friends and penitents must not be deprived of the last lesson he would give, the lesson of a Christian death. First, those nearest and dearest to him of the number were admitted; then came a succession of priests, the Cardinal Archbishop and his coadjutor came to thank him for his labours in the diocese and to give him their blessing. One of his old patronage children, the young Abbé Fossin,

who came from Poitiers to take leave of him, had
the happiness of saying Mass in the chapel and of
giving the Bread of Life to his dying Father, and
so the apostle of the Paris boys and of the young
seminarians received the last Viaticum at the hands
of one whom he had trained for the priesthood.
Then, by a silent and common consent, the doors of
his house were opened to all who desired to come.
At one time, when the last moment was thought
to be imminent and the prayers for the dying were
being recited, he lay so calm and motionless that
all thought that he was gone when the last
" Amen " was spoken; but just then he lifted up
his hands, and in a clear thrilling voice which none
who heard it ever forgot, spoke one word, *Alleluia!*
then, after " that cry of spiritual gladness which
was the expression of his whole life," as his brother
well says, he relapsed into silence and remained
motionless as before.   From that moment the room
was never empty; and the few words he said to
each in turn would show how perfectly he knew
them.

Among these last visits was that of the Abbé
Chaumont, one of his most beloved spiritual children, whose direction he esteemed so highly that
he had confided to him the care of his mother's soul.
On taking leave of him Mgr. de Ségur gave him a
very precious *souvenir*, the old wooden *prie-dieu* at
which his penitents had knelt for so many years.
Late in the evening his old secretary and Roman

convert, the Abbé Klingenhoffen, arrived from Poitiers for a few last words and the blessing which was given in a voice of thrilling tenderness. Almost his last visitor was M. Le Rebours, the excellent curé of the Madeleine, the companion of his early years and his life-long friend. Their parting was a most beautiful and Christian one; the Abbé bending over his · dying friend, spoke to him in the strong words of faith of his happiness in being so near Heaven, and begged him to pray for him there that, above all things, the grace of purity of intention might be his. Very clearly and distinctly Mgr. de Ségur replied: "Ah yes—purity of intention, that is everything!"

Nothing disturbed or distressed him; self-forgetful, and full of charity to the last, he allowed his face or hands to be kissed with an angelic smile, making the sign of the Cross over each in turn till his failing hand refused the office. Then M. Diringer begged him to rest, but he answered: "No, no, I will go on blessing them till there is an end of me" —*Jusqu'à ma complète démolition.* One of the joys of this last day was the blessing of the Holy Father, which he received twice; from the Nuncio and from Cardinal Chigi.

Night came, and he was alone with those who were to watch by him; among these was a young doctor, M. Ingigliardi, who had a singular and touching devotion to the "blind saint." He was bending over him, moistening his lips, and whisper-

ing the most affectionate words in his ear, when
suddenly he was assailed by a strange temptation
against the faith: "What," he asked himself, "if
this holy priest, after a life spent in the service of
God, should not be rewarded after death, what if
instead of the joys of heaven, his lot should be
annihilation?" Tortured by this involuntary doubt,
he said *in his heart only:* "O Monseigneur, will you
not come, after your death, to tell us that there is a
Heaven and that you are there?" The silent
question was answered—they were his last words—
"Believe, my son. O my child, believe!" At the
time, no one had the key to these words but he to
whom they were addressed, and to him they have
been the strength and consolation of his life.

As dawn broke on the morning of June 9, 1881,
Gaston de Ségur drew his last breath. The shadows
which had so long veiled the face of the earth from
his eyes had passed away for ever in the light of
the everlasting day, in which they opened to see the
face of the Master.

The Abbé Diringer, the faithful Méthol and his
wife and children remained with the Ségur family
through the night beside all that was earthly of
their saintly brother, friend and master.

His devoted medical attendant, Dr. Ingigliardi,
stood for three hours after closing his eyes, with one
hand on the forehead, the other under the chin of
his dead friend and father, till the features had
become rigid in death, praying silently all the time,

with his eyes fixed on the face he so loved and venerated. The only thing he asked for in return for his services was some linen cloths which had been applied to Mgr. de Ségur's leg which was painfully inflamed in his last illness, "they are relics," he said, "which will cure some of my patients."

While this devoted friend was thus watching by the body, another, the Abbé Diringer, was offering the Holy Sacrifice for the soul, in the chapel where he whom they mourned had so often offered the same spotless Victim, where he had spent so many hours of intercession and reparation. One can well understand the feeling of mingled sorrow and thanksgiving with which, as his brother tells us, that Mass was heard by all present, and how they felt that the souls of his mother and sister were even then welcoming him to that glorious Eternity where assuredly the works of him who had so blessedly "died in the Lord" had followed him.

During the four days that elapsed before the body of Mgr. de Ségur was taken to the church of St. Thomas d'Aquin, from dawn to nightfall the Rue du Bac was blocked by carriages and foot-passengers, and the room where he lay was full of visitors who after praying by the corpse, passed into the chapel and so out of the house. All was orderly and solemn; even those who came from mere curiosity left the presence of the dead with very different feelings; but they were few indeed,

and the crowds who pressed around the little iron
bedstead to kiss the feet, bare, like those of the
glorioso poverello to whose Third Order he belonged,
were true mourners.

On the morning of the 13th, Masses went on in
the chapel without interruption till the coffin was
taken away; then the last Host was consumed and
the tabernacle remained empty; in the words of
the Marquis, " God and His faithful servant left the
house in which they had dwelt for twenty-five years,
at the same moment." The funeral procession was,
as Mgr. de Ségur had enjoined, without all show or
pomp of any kind; but the love and reverence of
the people of Paris made it a solemn triumph, as
it passed through dense crowds, bare-headed and
silent, or only speaking in whispers, as in a church.
And what a *cortège* it was! there seemed no end to
the long lines of working men, apprentices and poor
women and children. The church was densely
crowded; the Requiem was a simple Low Mass—
this, too, by his own desire—but never had more
touching music been heard, for Gounod had begged
to play the organ during the ceremony, and the
exquisite subdued strains which filled the church
seemed the language of mingled sorrow, hope
and joy.

On the 16th the coffin was taken to Brittany, to
its last resting-place in the churchyard of Pluneret,
near Sainte-Anne-d'Auray. Mgr. de Ségur had
chosen it because " it is one of the places where the

dead are most prayed for," and also because his mother lay there. It had been a delight to him to plant and adorn the corner which he chose for the family burying-ground. This is described as singularly bright as well as devotional; a light railing encloses a space large enough for twelve graves, in the middle is a statue of our Lady of Lourdes, on her right St. Francis of Assisi, on her left St. Francis of Sales. There, by his mother's side, under a simple slab and cross of the blue granite of the country, the body of Gaston de Ségur waits for the morning of the Resurrection. On the cross are these words, "Jesus my Life and my Love," and on the stone—

AVE MARIA, GRATIA PLENA—IMMACULATA DEIPARA.

Here rests, in the peace of our Lord Jesus Christ, Louis Gaston de Ségur, priest, prelate of the Holy Roman Church, Episcopal-canon of the Chapter of Saint-Denys; in the Third Order of St. Francis Brother Francis-Mary of the Blessed Sacrament, born in Paris, April 15, 1820; died in Paris, June 9, 1881. *In Pace*—Jesus Deus, Propitius Esto Mihi Peccatori.

And so, as his brother says, "the last word he wrote of himself is the word *sinner*, and the last lesson which he teaches from the grave is humility."

The Marquis de Ségur, in the spirit of submission and reserve which stamps every word of his in touching on matters as to which the Church has not pronounced, alludes in a very few words to the "graces and cures obtained after special invocation and ascribed to the intercession of the 'blind saint,' which have from time to time rejoiced the hearts of his family and friends;" but he cannot refuse himself the pleasure of giving the following account sent to him by one of the pious Bretons of Pluneret.

The curiosity of strangers is excited by seeing little bags filled with earth hanging to the cross on Mgr. de Ségur's grave, and they ask what this means. They are hung there out of gratitude. In this part of Morbihan the workmen and field-labourers are very subject to fever, and they have the pious custom of praying for a cure through the intercession of persons who have led a very holy life. What they do is to take some of the blessed earth from the grave, and fill with it a little bag which they wear about them : then when the fever is gone, the bag is placed on the grave of the person invoked. Already the sepulchre of him whom Christian France and the Church mourn for is glorious . . . Peasants and great ladies, workmen and persons of high rank, young men of the world and priests, sometimes from a great distance, come in succession, not, as the saintly prelate begged in his humility, to pray for his soul, but to implore his intercession with God.

We conclude these short notices of a beautiful and saintly life, as his biographer concludes the memoir from which they are taken, by the last will and testament, written at Mgr. de Ségur's dictation a few months before his death.

✠

This is the expression of my last wishes. In the Name of the Father, and of the Son, and of the Holy Ghost; in the Name of our Lord Jesus Christ.

I die, as I have lived, in the faith of the Holy, Catholic, Apostolic, Roman Church, and in absolute submission to the Holy Apostolic See and all its decisions, in the love of the most Holy Sacrament of the Altar and of the Sacred Heart of Jesus, and with filial affection to the Blessed and Immaculate Virgin Mary and her holy mother St. Anne.

I die in the hope of the Divine mercy and under the special protection of my dear patrons, the Archangels St. Michael and St. Gabriel, SS. Peter and Paul, SS. Joseph and John the Evangelist, SS. Francis of Assisi, Francis of Sales, and Louis.

I die hoping to rejoin in the presence of God all whom I have loved and who have loved me on earth, especially my beloved mother and father, my sister Jane Frances, and my true father, the great and saintly Pope Pius the Ninth.

If, in any of my writings the least thing should be found opposed to the teaching, present or future, of the Holy See, I retract and condemn it with my whole heart. I wish to be buried in the habit of the Third Order of St. Francis of Assisi, barefoot, in token of poverty, with the blue scapular of the Immaculate Conception and that of the Sacred Heart; in my purple cassock, as a mark of my dependence on the

Pope and the Roman Church; in an alb and white chasuble, in token of my deep love for the Blessed Sacrament and for our Lady, and of my firm faith in the Resurrection. I wish the holy Gospels, the crucifix blessed and indulgenced by Pius the Ninth, and my rosary to be laid on my breast.

My heart is to be embalmed and then laid before the Blessed Sacrament in the Visitation Convent where my sister Sabine had the happiness of living and dying, and where my mother's heart also lies: I beg the dear and good sisters of the Visitation to allow my poor heart to be placed amongst them, in perpetual adoration before the Blessed Sacrament, and that it may have a share in all the prayers and Communions of the Community. On the leaden case containing my heart are to be engraved these words: " Jesus, my God, I love Thee and adore Thee with all my heart, in the Blessed Sacrament of the Altar."

I beg there may be no show or useless expense at my funeral. Wherever I die, I desire that there may be a simple Low Mass, with twelve candles round my coffin, six on each side and a thirteenth at the head as the rubric directs. . . .

I bless with the deepest fatherly affection all my spiritual children and all the Communities in which I have had the happiness of regularly exercising my ministerial office, especially the Seminaries of Montmorillon, Séez, Ste-Anne-d'Auray, and the little Congregation of Saint-Sulpice.

For the last time and with great affection I bless the Collège Stanislas and the Association of apprentices of Saint-Thomas-d'Aquin and all the children and young men whom I have directed and who are so dear to me, and in parting from them for a time, I urge upon them three things, the observance of which will be for their welfare and happiness: 1. To cherish throughout their lives a real love for the authority of the Holy Father: 2. a great practical love for the Blessed Sacrament and for Holy Communion: 3. a tender and filial affection to the Queen of Purity, Our Blessed Lady. I beg them always to remember their poor father in their prayers and Communions, and of those who have the happiness of being priests I ask a perpetual *memento* at the *Nobis quoque peccatoribus*.

I particularly bless, throughout their lives, all the members of our family, all my nephews and nieces and their children, I conjure them all never to forsake the service of God, to lead Christian lives, and always and in all things to be humbly submissive to the doctrine, the orders and the cause of the Vicar of Jesus Christ.

I hope that the grace of a priestly and a religious vocation, having once entered our family, may never be withdrawn from it, but that, to the end, it may enjoy the distinguished honour and the exceeding happiness of giving priests and religious to Our Lord and His Church. I commend myself with great confidence to the prayers of all the good and faithful Associates of Saint Francis of Sales, and I beg of them, after my death, to labour with redoubled zeal and devotion for the interests of the Faith and extension of the holy work. St. Francis of Sales will repay a hundredfold all that they may do for his Association.

I make the same request to all my brothers and sisters of the Third Order of St. Francis, that they may be its worthy members and true apostles.

I humbly beg pardon of our Lord and of all whom I may have disedified or scandalized in my miserable life, for all the evil I have done in any possible way; and I thank, with affectionate gratitude, all those who have done me good, corporal or spiritual, recommending my poor soul to their prayers.

I forgive, with my whole heart and for the love of Our Lord Jesus Christ, every one who may have injured me in the course of my life, or caused me any trouble, small or great. I hope that God will, in His goodness, vouchsafe to pardon all the calumnies which may have been directed against me.

And now, blessing my God for His countless mercies and graces, for my holy vocation, *for my blindness*, for the good He has enabled me to do, and for the evil He has taught me to avoid; blessing all whom I love, and in peace with all the world, I give up my soul into the Hands of my Saviour; I place it in His Sacred and Adorable Heart, and I desire to breathe my last breath and to commit my Eternity to the blessed and Immaculate Virgin, Mother of grace and Queen of Heaven.

May my dear Father, Saint Francis, and my dear patron, friend and protector, Saint Francis of Sales obtain for me the grace of a good death, and bring me themselves into the Presence of Our Lord Jesus Christ.

The second of September 1880, the twenty-sixth anniversary of the most blessed day on which I became blind.

✠ LOUIS GASTON DE SEGUR.